Entwined Publishing books by Rachael Heinan & Kimberly Metcalf

Amber Falls
Yours, Always
Forever Yours
Inevitably Yours

I0527706

Amber Falls

INEVITABLY YOURS

RACHAEL HEINAN & KIMBERLY METCALF

ENTWINED PUBLISHING

Inevitably Yours
ISBN # 978-1-80250-248-0
©Copyright Rachael Heinan & Kimberly Metcalf
Cover Art by Kelly Martin ©Copyright June 2025
Interior text design by Entwined Publishing
Published by Entice, an Entwined Publishing imprint

Published in 2025 by Entwined Publishing, United Kingdom.

Entwined Publishing is a division of Totally Entwined Group Limited.

INEVITABLY YOURS

Dedication

Rachael
Thank you to everyone else who has given me unwavering support: Pat, Isaac, Dan, Molly, Tim, and Amy. For Tim, we miss you.

Kimberly
To my family: Dad, Michele, Rich, Jami, Mike, Andrea, Paul and Laura. Thank you for your encouragement and support.

Chapter One

In business one of two things happen—you win or
you lose—and Sebastian Locke did not lose. Everything
he touched turned to gold, his intuition was
impeccable, and it had served him well. That intuition
was how he'd found himself in Amber Falls,
Massachusetts. As he sat behind his desk at the Amber
Falls Bee listening to this vexing woman rail on him for
yet another decision she didn't agree with, he thought
just once, maybe his intuition had been wrong.

"Sir, are you even listening to me?" Annabelle
Winters, star reporter at the Bee, made an exasperated
noise.

He closed his eyes, allowing himself brief respite.

"Sir, I have a million other things to do to get ready
for the Summer Solstice. I don't have time to watch you
take a cat nap."

"Winters." Sebastian opened his eyes. "Name one
thing that's important enough to warrant my
attention."

"Peach pie."

Sebastian's mouth went dry. Together, the words described a delightful dessert. Separately, each word formed carnal images in his head and once he saw that picture floating around, peach pie would never be the same to him again. He'd known this was coming for months, that the town would have a peach pie bake-off, and he, in a small corner of the soul he'd never admit he had, was looking forward to this one seasonal celebration. He was from Georgia, and any good Georgian knew peach pie, dammit.

Annabelle slammed a paper on his desk, breaking him from his thoughts. "The blurb on the peach pie bake-off is just one of the items you need to approve for the layout. I have the Summer Solstice activity schedule that needs to get printed, and I need your signature to approve the outline."

Sebastian leaned back in his chair and stretched his legs out to rest on the top of his desk, crossing his ankles. He picked up the folder and flipped through it as if he had all the time in the world. Which he did — one of the perks of being the boss. But they had this conversation every three months, going over in minute detail each of the seasonal festivals Amber Falls held. Not wanting to have the same talk today, he picked up the pen and signed his name on the dotted line.

"Have a good night, Winters." He flipped the folder onto the desk and closed his eyes once again.

"What?"

Sebastian counted to five before he forced his eyes back open. "You wanted the approval, and now you have it."

Annabelle was visibly stunned at his change in attitude. In months past, they'd had vehement arguments about the tiniest details of the previous festivals. It appeared that he didn't wear acquiescence well.

"You always have something you make fun of. Just like you did for the Fall Festival and Winter Wonderland." It seemed like Spring Fling had just finished, and Sebastian was already sick of the anticipation the whole town had over the Summer Solstice Celebration.

"Winters, are you going to argue with me now about my not arguing?"

He lifted the folder and offered the approved layout to her again.

Annabelle narrowed her eyes at him, distrust clear on her face. "Don't you want to know who plays in the softball game? Or what happens if no one shows up?"

He set the folder down and decided to see where this went. "Go on."

"Whoever wants to. We meet on the field the morning of the game and choose teams. Before you ask, if there aren't enough people, the adults grill and the kids play in the park."

He sat in silence, willing his cheek not to twitch with amusement.

"You don't want to know who chooses the movie for the outdoor movie night?"

Gesturing with his hand, he indicated she should proceed.

"City council does. Next will come a lewd, adolescent joke about how the peach pie is delivered for judging. After which I roll my eyes and you tell me how ludicrous the whole process is, that this town is wasting time and assets that could be better spent elsewhere."

Annabelle stopped and held his gaze. He took this opportunity to look at her, to check her out. Not a leer,

9

he was better than that, but an intense once-over — the kind he *shouldn't* give his subordinate.

To call Annabelle pretty would be a gross understatement. She was gorgeous. The kind of gorgeous that should be reserved for classical paintings, but the *Birth of Venus* had nothing on the Pique of Annabelle. She was a short spitfire and Sebastian was a tall man who topped her by a foot — less when she decided to wear skyscraper heels, which she often did. Her hair was an iridescent auburn that glinted a deep blue in the right light, but it was always up, never unbound, so he didn't know its length. Her features were small and fit her face.

"Winters, you've just made my point for me." He slid the folder over to her.

"I know you don't get why these festivals are important to Amber Falls, but why do you have to give me a hard time every time I need the approval for one of the layouts?"

"I'd like to point out, I did sign the layout upon your first request. And I'm not giving you a hard time, I'm giving you shit. There's a difference."

"I fail to see what that difference is."

"If I were to give you a hard time, I'd have you explain in detail why each of these activities is necessary to mark the Summer Solstice, because I can guarantee you that the season will turn to summer even if no" — he opened the folder back up — "flea market marks the occasion. Fall came, winter came, and spring has sprung, and you celebrated it with a damn May Day Festival. It all happened and will continue to happen for the rest of time."

"Then why does it make a difference how we celebrate it?" Annabelle sat in the chair across from Sebastian and propped her legs up on the desk in the same way his were. He raised his eyebrows at her with her movement, but she didn't remove them. "We all know the seasons continue to change and time marches on, but what's so wrong with wanting to embrace those changes and be present in those moments? These are the things I remember from my childhood, the moments I remember with family and friends — the lazy days of summer vacation when there wasn't a care in the world other than staying up late to watch the baseball game or my dad counting the time between lightning and thunder during storms with me."

"I've never said I don't understand why it happens and what the town is trying to accomplish, I've just stated that there are better things to spend time and money on."

"That's not how you've portrayed it," Annabelle responded.

"Yes, well, there it is. And that's why I'll be running for mayor."

They looked at each other for another beat then Annabelle stood so fast she almost knocked her chair over and pointed toward the door.

"Get out. Go home, pack your bags and leave town."

Sebastian laughed. "Calm down, Winters, I'm joking." He could see the pink blush starting to creep along her neckline. He did enjoy getting a rise out of her. "I don't need anything else tying me to this town."

"I don't have time for your bad jokes, sir." Annabelle gathered her notebook and folders from his desk. "Don't you own your house? Isn't that the definition of putting down roots?"

Smirking, he replied, "No, that's just a good investment."

"If you don't need anything else, I'm going to leave for the night." She stood waiting, the tip of one stiletto tapping on the floor.

"I needed to ask you about one more thing." He gestured to the chair and Annabelle sat once more. He could see her fidgeting with the edge of the folder, now on her lap. "What's your rush this evening, Winters? Hot date?"

Her half grin was that of a sly fox. "If you must pry into my personal life, yes, I do have a date, and I'm already running behind. What can I help you with?"

His stomach flopped at her admission, and he stopped himself from asking any more questions. "My sister, Sofia, is coming to stay with me for a while this summer. I want to make sure she's comfortable and has what she needs to, how did you put it, be in the moment."

"Careful, sir, I might start to think you have a heart. Besides, don't you just go home on the weekends and plug into the wall like a Roomba? What could I possibly help you with."

"Winters, please." This was as close as he'd get to begging. "Prudence is busy and I could use some help making sure I have whatever she might need during her stay."

Several moments passed before she answered. "Are you saying I was your last choice?"

Undeterred, he responded, "Of course you were."

Annabelle got up and walked to the door. She'd laid one hand on the doorknob when she paused, turning back to face him. "As it should be. I want it noted that I'm only agreeing to this because I wouldn't mind a favor from Sebastion Locke in my back pocket. When does she get in?"

"On Sunday."

"Fine, I'll be at your house Saturday morning." She turned on her heel and left his office, shutting the door gently, compared to her usual slam.

Sebastian shuffled paperwork on his almost empty desk until he heard the front door to the Bee close. Slumping back in his chair, he took a fortifying breath. He wasn't sure how to best describe his relationship with Annabelle. Their relationship, or lack thereof, wasn't love/hate, more like hate/hate, or love to hate.

His mind wandered back to a few years ago in Atlanta and the reason he'd passed on a novel submitted to him by one Annabelle Winters, before she'd been an intern at his family's company, Locke Communications. He hadn't felt it. Nothing about it had been fresh or new. On top of that, she'd submitted a romance novel and romance wasn't his…thing.

The decision to reject her novel had plagued him since he'd landed in Amber Falls. As he sat behind his desk, he thought maybe he'd been wrong just once in his life. He let his mind continue to wander around the memories from years ago. He might have used the words trite and mediocre. The words derivative and execrable might have slipped out before he'd given her a harsh rejection.

Would it have been worth it? To not listen to his gut for one time in his life to have peace now?

Yes. In the deep recesses of his black heart, doubt crept in. Just once he should've taken the hit, reputation be damned.

A loud knock sounded at his office door, and he jumped in surprise. "Come in."

"Hey, boss." One of the newspaper's columnists walked into his office. "I'm about done for the night. Is there anything else you need?"

"Peter, you went on a date with Winters, right?"

Peter shrugged. "I wouldn't call it a date. She ended up being more preoccupied by someone else on New Year's Eve, if I recall."

Oh, Sebastian recalled. He recalled her dress cut so low he swore when she moved a certain way her areolas showed, and he recalled her biting words, digging into him every time he spoke that night. Devlin Watkins and Gabe Atwood, two of their mutual friends, had reunited that evening and the drama that followed was worthy of a front-page spread in *Person* magazine. What he remembered most, though, was walking Annabelle to Devlin's after Devlin had run off in a panic when she'd seen Gabe. Devlin lived above her coffee shop, Books and Beans, two doors down from Gabe's bar, Finnegan's. Midnight had passed and Annabelle had been preparing to leave to see if Devlin was okay. Leaving Sofia at the bar, he'd informed Annabelle he was walking her over, despite her protestations.

Annabelle had had plenty to drink that night, and had rocked a bit on her heels as he'd held the door open for them to exit, catching the tip of her shoe on the landing. She'd reached out, in what he could only assume was knee-jerk reaction, and grabbed his hand to steady herself. What surprised him most was that she hadn't let go for the twenty or so feet it took to get to Devlin's door. They'd stood at the entrance to Devlin's loft, Annabelle swaying and Sebastian standing motionless, afraid that if he moved she'd break her intense gaze. He'd lowered his head, eyes now transfixed on her plump lips, and he was a hair's breadth away, the warm puff of her breath warming his cold lips, when a raucous group of drinkers from Finnegan's burst out of the bar and the moment was broken. Annabelle had turned and unlocked Devlin's door, retreating inside, and it closed with a resounding thud.

Devlin and Gabe were now exclusive, and Sebastian and Annabelle hadn't spoken of that night since.

"Boss?" Peter interrupted his thoughts. "You still with me?"

"Sorry, Peter." Sebastian shook his head to clear his thoughts.

"That was the one and only time we went out and I think we were in each other's company for maybe ten minutes total. That's okay, though, makes things less awkward around here."

"You had your eyes set on my sister, didn't you?"

"Um, so anyway, you need me for anything else?"

Sebastian wasn't about to let him off easy. He liked watching people squirm. "What piece are you working on?"

"Annabelle has—has me—" He stuttered at Sebastian's raised eyebrows and corrected himself. "*I'm* working on this month's births layout."

"How many storks flew into Amber Falls this last month?"

"Twenty-one babies were born this month."

Sebastian whistled. "That's more than usual. The town has been busy."

"We had an unseasonable cold snap in August, right before you got here. We always have extra births nine months after those."

A cold front had moved through that foretold Sebastian's arrival. He liked that imagery.

He waved his hand toward the door. "You can go. I'm about done here myself."

"All right, boss, I'll see you tomorrow."

Sebastian was once again alone in his office and a now familiar feeling crept over him. It had come out of nowhere a few weeks ago. He'd never been restless before. Since he was a child, he'd known what he was supposed to do. He had an innate sense of internal direction, one that pointed him to his true north at every turn and was propelled forward by this.

He reached up and loosened his tie, a tightness there that wouldn't go away even with the release of his shirt's top button. He wasn't restless to *leave* Amber Falls, and that was the part that was confusing him. The obvious assumption would be that this small town had gotten under his skin to the point where he needed to get out. To go far away from the festivals and the baby announcements and the peach pies. But he'd made friends here, friends he had more of a bond with than the trust fund cohorts he grew up with.

And the newspaper. Locke Communications was in the business of publishing and they had never owned a paper before *The Amber Falls Bee*, and Sebastian found that he was enjoying running it. Branching out into a world that was considered a dying business wasn't easy, but these small newspapers were holding on. They were holding on despite all odds and that had a lot to do with the locals.

The *locals*. That was a loaded term. Sebastian had become friends with a handful of people born and raised in Amber Falls. Other than Gabe and Devlin, he'd met Prudence Hardwick, an interior designer, and her fiancé, Greyson Atwood, the retired movie star. Devlin was a recent transplant to Amber Falls, much like himself, but the others had known each other since they were kids. The link that connected them all was Annabelle.

He straightened out his desk while he contemplated where life had taken him. Atlanta was where he grew up and was also the headquarters of Locke Communications. Before that he'd gone where he was told —

New York, Boston, Paris, London—anywhere the company was acquiring something or trying to build into emerging markets. His youth had been shaped by boarding schools and his adulthood by his job. He didn't want to paint a bad picture, though. He was closer to his family than most people with his same upbringing and for that he was grateful.

Where did Amber Falls fit into all of this? A small town with a thriving college scene didn't seem like any place that an up-and-coming thirty-something would find themselves, but here he was, approving birth announcements and thinking ahead to when the next dart night would be.

His eyebrows crinkled in confusion. Was Sebastian becoming a...local? Was he on the same level as Mrs. Crenshaw, everyone's favorite nosy neighbor? He shuddered at the thought while the simultaneous thought popped into his head that becoming an Amber Falls local wouldn't be the worst thing that ever happened to him.

Chapter Two

Annabelle hadn't been on a date in…well…it had been in this decade at least, but she preferred not to think about how long. This particular date was one Prudence Hardwick, her best friend, had been pestering her to go on for months.

"Don't roll your eyes at me, Annabelle," Prudence blazed.

"We're not on a video call, how would you know if I'm rolling my eyes?"

"I can tell. I can always tell."

Prudence had a gift for reading situations.

"I was just stretching my eyes."

"Well, get your head in the game. Troy's a very eligible bachelor and he thinks you're cute."

"Cute? I'm not a doll."

"Yes, I know that." Prudence sighed. "Why can't you let yourself be excited about this?"

Annabelle was on her way to meet her date and her steps faltered as the image of a too-tall media mogul flashed through her mind. The image was quick, in and out before she knew it, but there it was, and she shook her head to clear it out. She was excited about this date. Troy Bolson was a catch. If the fire department had a calendar, he'd be on the front. More than once she'd enjoyed his company, at charity events or out with mutual friends.

"I *am* excited about this, Pru," Annabelle insisted.

"I hope you are. Troy was the one that got me out of the tree when I rescued Mrs. Crenshaw's cat, and if Grey hadn't come home when he did, I very well might have gone after him myself."

"You would've done no such thing. You and Grey are soulmates and even a red-hot fireman wouldn't have stopped you from getting together."

Greyson Atwood was a retired actor. He'd spent years in Hollywood making himself a household name before returning to his hometown of Amber Falls to win the love of Prudence.

"You need to go out with someone. I was starting to think you were waiting to see if Sebastian would ask you out."

"Sebastian, my boss?"

"Do we know another Sebastian?" Prudence questioned.

"I wish you and Devlin would knock it off about him. We just work together."

The silence on the other end of the line spoke volumes.

"Mmhm," came the not so convinced reply.

"He did ask me to come out to his house and help him get ready for his sister's visit, with some lame excuse that you were busy."

"Well, we are busy. I haven't said anything yet, but I think Grey and I will have to go to Los Angeles soon for some business stuff, but I'm not sure when."

"You still could've helped him."

"Nah, I'd rather hear all the stories about how you two almost killed each other."

"Pru," Annabelle warned.

"Okay, okay, I'll stop it. We need to focus on Troy anyway."

"What do you know about him?" Annabelle asked.

"What else do you need to know aside from the fact you could grate cheese on his abs?"

"So shallow."

"He was able to carry me down from a tree, so he's strong," Prudence added.

"You're not that big, Pru. Besides, everyone is bigger than me, I'm about the size of a teacup. I'd much rather be an Amazon like you."

"If he can carry me, just imagine what he can do with you."

Annabelle had nothing wrong with her imagination—in fact, it had been overactive as of late and she needed to rein it in. Or did she? Maybe Troy was just the diversion she needed.

"What do you know about him *besides* his physical attributes?"

"That's for you to find out, my dear. He's just eye candy to me."

"I'm almost there anyway. In fact I think I see him waiting outside." In the distance she saw a tall, well-built man dressed in the casual outfit of a firefighter—tight blue khakis and a tucked in T-shirt with the department's logo on it. His hair was so blond it was almost white.

"Tell him hi, and I'm doing well."

Annabelle laughed. "I'm sure he'll want to know all about how you're doing, Pru."

"You never know," Prudence huffed. "Just because I'm engaged doesn't mean I'm dead."

"I'm just joking," Annabelle placated. "Call me in twenty?"

"You won't need an emergency call twenty minutes into your date."

"You have to, just in case it goes downhill."

"Fine, I'll talk to you in a bit, bye!"

The line clicked off and Annabelle slowed her pace, passing by the Bee's building as she crossed the street, taking in more of Troy now that she was closer to him. He was standing with his back to her, studying the awning over the restaurant door.

He turned around and she saw a notebook and pencil in his hand.

"I wouldn't stand under that if I was you," he cautioned, moving her to the side of the door.

"What?" *He didn't even say hi.*

"This is a death trap waiting to happen. That awning is only secured to the building with six anchors. Fire code calls for at least eight." He jotted something else down in his book and closed it with a flourish. "Don't worry, I'll open the door and you can rush through."

Annabelle stood and stared at him holding the door open trying to act like some kind of knight in shining armor, protecting her from certain doom.

"Thanks?" she questioned. He hustled her through the door with an impatient gesture.

They stood at the front of the restaurant waiting for a seat, an uncomfortable silence settling over them. At least Annabelle found the silence uncomfortable, she wasn't sure that Troy remembered she was there, he was so busy writing in his notebook, muttering about the restaurant's perceived lack of cleanliness.

"Um, I thought you were a fireman. Aren't there other city offices that deal with this?"

"Hey, 'see something say something' isn't just for suspicious people walking down the street. I'm constantly keeping an eye out for any kind of code violation."

And this, ladies and gentleman, is why he's still single.

Once they were led to the table, he at least pulled her chair out for her, but stopped her from sitting when he jiggled it around.

"The chair is weak," he stated. "The wrong person sits on it, and it'll turn to kindling."

"At least you'd be here to put any fires out," she joked.

"Fires are no laughing matter, Annabelle. A place like this would go up in a few minutes and the damage would be catastrophic."

"I'm not going to break the chair, Troy. Can I just sit?"

"Of course, it's your choice."

Annabelle took a deep breath as she sat, kicking herself for choosing this restaurant for their date. Although, she believed that any place she chose would have been just as eviscerated by Troy. Still, she was determined to enjoy herself. Or at least have some stories she could tell for years to come.

"How old were you when you learned about Smoky the Bear?" he asked.

Nope. Not gonna happen. She looked at her watch. Five minutes. Only five minutes had passed, Prudence wasn't going to call for fifteen more and they hadn't gotten drinks yet.

"Smoky the who?" She knew that he'd find no humor in anything she said, but she did it anyway.

His face fell and she swore she saw his lip quivering. "You don't know who Smoky the Bear is?"

"I've heard of Paddington." She was going to hell.

She was saved from being shamed by him when the server arrived.

"I'll have a whiskey, neat," she ordered.

"Really, hard liquor with dinner?"

She exchanged a pained look with the waitress. "Make it a double."

An eternity passed before her phone rang. It had been the longest forty minutes of her life.

"Hello?"

"I'm so sorry, AB! I was distracted and lost track of time."

"Get it done with and come back to bed," she heard Greyson say in the background.

She held her hand over the phone and whispered to Troy, "Sorry, it's my boss," then spoke back into the receiver. "There was a double murder?"

"I said I was sorry!" Prudence wailed.

"It took forty minutes for police to arrive after they claimed they'd be there in twenty?"

"I'll make it up to you, I promise."

"In that case I'd better come right in." Annabelle shook her head at Troy and made a sad face.

"Wow! That bad?"

"You're right, it's unbelievable how quick things can take a turn for the worse."

"Tell me about it tomorrow, okay?"

"The police chief will show them no mercy, I'm sure of it." She pressed the end button on her screen harder than she should have.

"Did you say double murder?" Troy's eyes were like saucers.

Oh shit. "No, that's just newspaper speak for…um… two stories dropping at once."

"Oh, okay." He didn't look convinced.

The bell on the restaurant door jingled and Troy glanced over. Annabelle groaned when Sebastian entered, before turning it into a cough.

"Isn't that your boss right there?" Troy questioned.

Sebastian's eyes met Annabelle's then darted to Troy. The smallest smirk appeared on his lips and he sauntered over.

"When you said you had a work emergency, I didn't imagine your boss coming to get you." Troy nodded to Sebastian as he reached them.

Sebastian's eyes widened and Annabelle threw him a silent plea to go along with it. His eyes crinkled in the corners, and she knew she'd have to pay a hefty price for whatever happened next.

"Of course," Sebastian drawled after making her squirm. "I was wondering what was taking you so long, Winters, and I figured I'd have to come drag you back into the office."

"Sorry, sir, I just got the call," she trailed off. "From you."

They sat in silence while Troy tossed a suspicious glance between the two.

"Yes, well, the newspaper is just across the street, and I was already coming over here when I called. I knew you'd drag your feet, even though this is of the upmost importance. Let's go," he barked.

Startled, Annabelle jumped out of her seat, almost knocking it over and grabbed her purse. The chair *was* quite rickety.

"I'm so sorry, Troy, duty calls," she apologized.

Troy followed them to the door, holding it open so they could pass through, eying the dangerous awning the whole time. "I was having a good time, I hope we can do this again?"

Annabelle didn't know what to say, but there was no way he was dense enough to think she'd go out with him again. She could sense the amusement wafting off Sebastian.

"I'm sorry, Troy, I have so much going on right now, as you can see by this work emergency, that I'm finding I don't have enough time for dating. I hope you understand."

Disappointment crossed his features. "I understand. Say hi to Prudence for me, will you?"

"I will." She waved as she and Sebastian walked across the street to the Bee. He settled his hand at the small of her back as he'd been doing lately, his touch featherlight, but still there.

"Will you come in with me?" Annabelle pleaded once they reached their offices. "He'll think it's odd if you don't."

"I don't know, Winters. I haven't eaten yet and I'm not sure I can wait much longer."

She narrowed her eyes at him. "I'll buy you dinner if you wait until he's gone."

He nodded. "You've got yourself a deal."

They stood in the foyer of the Bee, watching through the window as Troy pulled out his notepad and started writing again. After a few minutes he still hadn't gone back into the restaurant and the longer Troy wrote, the more Annabelle became aware of Sebastian's presence. He was still touching her lower back and the warmth from his hand spread into her as they stood.

"What is he doing?" Annoyance clearly laced his voice.

"Writing citations."

"You're joking."

She turned to face him. They were much closer than she'd anticipated, but she couldn't step away as her back was now against the door.

"I'm not. He was either writing fire code violations or complaining about the things he couldn't cite them for the whole time we were there."

"I get taking your job seriously, but he must be miserable company. No wonder he's single."

"If you're single, you're miserable, is that right? What does that say about us?"

Sebastian flashed a grin. "Misery loves company." He moved back and peered out of the door once again. "Citation boy has gone in, I'm sure he'll try to shut the whole place down."

"That's too much power for one person."

"I don't want to admit it, but I think you're right. Now, let's go get dinner."

Annabelle raised her eyebrows. It would be a cold day in hell before she sat through a meal with him. Group meals, work meals, those were fine, but one on one with no buffer or pretense of work? She knew they'd be at each other's throats within minutes, and she'd rather do almost anything else.

"I wasn't serious." She rustled in her bag as she spoke. "I'm already helping you get ready for your sister's visit, that's enough outside of work time." Finding a twenty-dollar bill, she held it out to him. "I agreed to pay, but you're on your own."

His eyes held hers for a moment longer than was comfortable before he snatched the twenty from her and opened the door. "I'll walk you home, I'm going that way."

She ran through the list of restaurants they'd pass on her way home and she decided he could be telling the truth. She was tired and didn't want to argue with him, so they started off down the sidewalk.

"So," Sebastian started after they'd walked a few blocks. "That was your hot date?"

"Yes," Annabelle confirmed. "He rescued both Prudence and Mrs. Crenshaw's cat last fall when Pru went up into a tree to get Billy Bones."

"She actually climbed up the tree?"

"Prudence will do anything to help someone."

Annabelle searched for something to say. She wasn't used to being alone with Sebastian and if they ever were, a fight was sure to break out. Over the last few months things had changed between them, though.

In January they'd gone to Greyson and Gabe's family cabin high up in the mountains where cell reception was nonexistent. Annabelle had seen the stress melt away from Sebastian at the cabin. He'd been a different man. Well, not altogether different—his reliable arrogance had still been there—but the layer just underneath that, the one that he never uncovered to the world, had cracked through. Just enough that Annabelle had been able to see how overworked and exhausted he was.

She hadn't told anyone, but the first night at the cabin she'd crept into what was supposed to be Devlin's room to ask her if she had some extra face wash—she'd left hers at home—and had been beyond surprised to find Sebastian in the bed instead. His face had been smooth, no worry lines or cocky grin adorned it, and he'd looked so relaxed and peaceful that part of her heart had melted toward him. He'd so obviously been out to the world and she'd walked over without even realizing it and brushed a lock of hair off his forehead. He was a different man, young and carefree.

Getting angry at him had been harder since then, though not impossible — he *was* still Sebastian Locke.

"Believe it or not, that wasn't the worst first date I've been on," Annabelle admitted.

"I think your date trying to get the restaurant you're eating in closed down is pretty bad."

Annabelle shook her head. "I was in college and went to a concert with a guy from my psychology class. We'd been working in a study group together all semester and I thought he gave off all the signs that he was into me, so I was happy when he asked me out."

"A concert can't be that bad, unless he sacrificed you into a mosh pit."

"We got through the show just fine, but when I went to the bathroom afterward he disappeared. I wandered the venue for a half-hour, but he'd just left me there."

"He just took off?"

"Yep. I couldn't find a sign of him anywhere. Prudence had to come and pick me up."

"That must've been an awkward rest of the semester."

"You don't know the half of it. He pretended he had no clue what I was talking about the following Monday in class and made a big fuss to everyone that I was nuts."

Sebastian snorted. "That guy's got a lot of nerve to pull that."

"I got the last laugh," Annabelle explained. "I was able to find people from the same concert that had pictures of us at the show and made my final class project about gaslighting. He never saw it coming."

"That's amazing, Winters. What did he do?"

"Presentations were the last day of class and I never saw him again, but, man, was it vindicating. It wasn't worth my mental energy to care after that."

"That's a good attitude to have."

"What about you?" Annabelle asked. "Have you ever had a bad date, or has everything in your life been perfect?"

Sebastian looked offended. "Nothing is perfect in my life. I have as many ups and downs as a normal person."

"A normal person? That says it all right there." Annabelle decided to give him a break from her ribbing. "But really, what was your worst date?"

"A wedding."

"They're not ideal first dates, but it doesn't sound like the worst ever."

"She didn't tell me it was a wedding."

"No!"

"Yes. From what I gathered from others during the night, she got her kicks from taking her dates places they weren't expecting. I'm adventurous, but I also don't want to wake up in Taiwan one day with a missing kidney."

"I draw the line at organ removal," Annabelle agreed.

"I'm glad you have some standards, Winters."

Annabelle felt the sense of annoyance return. "Of course I have standards, sir."

"I'm just saying, the last few dates of yours that I've seen have had a severe lack of judgment on your part."

They'd ended up outside Annabelle's condo and had been standing in front of the entrance for a few minutes.

"My lack of judgment?" The now familiar tug of a smirk was just pulling at Sebastian's lips. "My judgment is sound, thank you very much. In fact, it's so good that you're eating alone tonight and I'm heading upstairs to relax." She yanked the outer door open and stormed in, but he caught it before it could shut.

"Wait! You're still coming out to help with Sofia's room, right?"

Lightning bolts flew out of her eyes, but she relented when she saw panic cross his face. "Yes. I'll be there, but you'd better change your attitude and be much less insulting of me." She pulled the door closed and moved toward the elevator.

Much less? How about not at all? Maybe her judgment wasn't so sound, after all.

Chapter Three

Sebastian didn't know why he did it. Needling Annabelle was so easy. She took offense at almost everything he said and once he saw the fire start to rise in her, he had an unnatural need to fan the flames, to see how high they could go, and he didn't mind getting burned in the process. He needed to rein in this impulse today. She wouldn't have anywhere to and he needed as much of her help as possible.

Sebastian's only sibling, Sofia, was coming to Amber Falls to visit. She'd visited for a few weeks at Christmas, which was more time they'd spent together in quite a while. After Sebastian moved to Atlanta to take his place as the head of Locke Communications, Sofia had come in and out of his life, dipping her toes in the publishing pool before flitting off to do something else, then coming back at the call of their father.

Over the last couple of years, she'd been working in their Boston office and once Sebastian had moved, they'd got together a few times. He was surprised she wanted to come back to Amber Falls. They'd always been close, but life had the habit of getting in the way of even the closest of families. The holidays had been her last visit, and he hadn't purchased his house then, so she'd stayed at a bed and breakfast. He had the extra room now and wanted her to stay with him, but this meant making sure his house was ready for a long-term guest.

Sebastian prided himself on his taste, but decorating was not his forte. Most of his apartments had been company-owned properties that had already been furnished. The house he'd bought in Amber Falls was the opposite of every stylistic choice he'd ever made. It had been a bungalow rental with furniture so old it could've had grandkids.

He'd asked both Prudence and Gabe to help him, but they'd both be out of town, so he'd had no choice but to turn to Annabelle. *Of course I had a choice.* He could've hired someone to finish the guest room, or done the work himself, but when he was in the office with Annabelle the words had just slipped out. Now, he was sitting on his front porch waiting for her to show up at his house.

She'd never been there before, and he was nervous. Why? He didn't know. Since his updates, the house was now perfectly presentable. Two bedrooms and two bathrooms, rounded out with a kitchen and living room. The place was small, but he didn't mind.

He was rearranging the porch furniture for the hundredth time when Annabelle pulled into his driveway. She stepped out of the sedan, her six-inch heels grinding into the gravel driveway. She slammed her door after she got out and took a long look at either the house or him, he couldn't tell, before removing her sunglasses and walking the rest of the way up the drive.

"I pictured it bigger," she stated.

"It's big enough, Winters, I've never had any complaints before."

"I'm talking about the house, sir."

"Of course you are," he drawled, and motioned with his hand for her to come up the steps. "What else would I be talking about?"

"One can never tell. I like the porch, it's quaint," she nodded to the two rocking chairs with a low table in between on one side and a hanging swing on the other.

"I spend most of my time out back. That porch is screened in, so fewer mosquitoes."

"Well, lead the way." Annabelle turned toward the door then stopped when he didn't move and waited, clearly expecting him to go inside.

She stopped too close, and he could smell her Dior perfume, but another smell assailed him, something under the fancy scent that he hadn't noticed before. He took a small sniff, trying to identify it, stepping back at the sharp turn of her head.

"Did you just smell me, Mr. Locke?"

"Allergies, Winters. I'm right across from a cornfield, if you haven't noticed." He opened the front door, allowing her to go in before him, the unknown scent tickling his nose as she walked by.

Annabelle stopped in the entryway and glanced around the small living room.

"Contemporary style, just like your office," she commented, running a hand over the leather of a large, tufted couch.

"This place was a rental before I bought it. Imagine the house filled with flowery couches, wicker end tables and so much wallpaper. It had a very 1980s Florida nursing home vibe. I knew I could update it quickly — it was one of the reasons I bought it." The way her small hand caressed the leather made him flush, and when her fingertips scratched over the fabric, all reason fled his brain and pooled in his cock. One simple motion had almost undone him. He blamed the intimacy of their location and rushed to lead her through a tiny kitchen to the back door. "This was the other reason."

They stepped out onto the screened porch and he heard her intake of breath. The porch was almost the same size as the house, and overlooked the lake. The sun shone off the lake's smooth surface, not a breeze rippling the water, surrounded by pine trees so thick that only the docks gave away the existence of other properties.

"This was the only house on the lake with a sandy beach. The others just have a boat slip. I knew it was small and not my taste, but as soon as I stepped out here, I knew I had to have it. I want to turn this into a year-round living space but haven't had the time yet." He let her take in the view before motioning outside. "Did you want to go down to the beach?"

Annabelle shrugged and slipped off her heels. He knew she was short, but topping out at his chest was very short, and she had to tilt her head up to speak.

"Let's go."

Sebastian opened the screen door, and they descended the steps to a rock pathway. When they reached the beach, he noticed her bright red toenails and narrow feet sinking into the sand and another tingle rushed through him. He didn't have a foot fetish, but he couldn't help but think about kissing those toes as she put her legs over his shoulders. She didn't stop at the water's edge, but walked right in, sighing when she stepped into the water.

"This is heaven." She swished her feet around then walked out a slight distance.

"On the days I'm home early enough from work, I bring a chair down here and watch the sun set."

"Is it naturally this sandy?" She pointed toward the shoreline to their right. "These small lakes can be mucky and have lots of weeds."

"I'm not sure what the previous owners did, but the sand has stayed nice since winter ended."

Annabelle turned and gestured toward him. "Come in, the water is perfect."

He gestured to his sneaker-clad feet and jeans. "I'm not as prepared as you are."

"Don't be annoying. Come in."

Before Sebastian knew it his shoes and socks were off, he'd rolled up his jeans and he was in the water standing next to Annabelle. She was like a siren that would lead him to his sure death. The water was cool, but not cold, and the sand sifted through his toes as he took a few more steps out. She followed, her hand brushing his as she came up next to him.

"Do you smell that?" she asked.

"Hm?" he intoned in way of response.

"The smell of pine trees was one thing I missed the most when I left here. Atlanta just doesn't have pine trees like this, so thick that light gets lost in them. The fresh smell can soak into your pores and cleanse out all the bad vibes."

Her head didn't reach his shoulder, and he leaned the tiniest bit toward her. He took the opportunity, under the guise of smelling pine trees, to take a deep breath, trying to pinpoint the scent of her, but it still eluded him.

"Bad vibes?" he questioned.

"Yeah, anything that eats away at your soul."

35

"That sounds like a horror movie."

"Anything that can eat away at your soul is horrific." Annabelle gave a little shiver despite the warmth of the sun. "Let's go get this room started."

A tug started deep inside him—the smallest little pull, but just enough to make him aware of its presence.

* * * *

"You weren't kidding me," Annabelle said, not more than an hour later. She held up the furniture instructions to his face. "Can you even read this?"

"It might be Swedish furniture, but the instructions are in English. I don't have the mind for instructions. I've tried."

They were sitting in the middle of the guest bedroom, pieces of furniture piled around them, no more set up than it was when they'd removed it from the packaging.

"Unbelievable," Annabelle muttered. "I thought you told me you were a Boy Scout?"

"I was, and I could build this furniture from scratch."

"Then why didn't you?"

"I thought this would save time."

She side-eyed him. "You mean you thought Prudence would put it all together for you."

"Prudence, Gabe, Grey—any of them would've done."

"I'll admit, I'm seeing an entirely different side to you."

"What's that supposed to mean?"

"So, you could've built your own furniture, but you waited until the day before your sister gets here to get someone to help you because you have a hard time reading instructions."

"I don't have a hard time, it's impossible."

"Gabe has his woodworking shop, why didn't you have him help you?"

"He's been too busy running Finnegan's and renovating both his and Devlin's shops. I didn't want to put any more pressure on him."

Devlin and Gabe both had purchased shops next to their downtown locations. Devlin to expand her coffee shop and Gabe to open a studio to display his woodworking.

"Besides," Sebastian continued, "he had one premade bed frame and I nabbed that for my room."

Annabelle smoothed out the instructions once more on the floor but popped her head up at this. "You have some of Gabe's furniture? He told me he didn't have any to sell yet."

"A bed and two nightstands."

"That jerk!"

"Oh, come off it, Winters. I needed a king-sized frame. You have, what, a twin?" He enjoyed the pursed annoyance of her lips.

"Yes, I'm a grown woman so obviously I still have a twin bed frame."

"I'm just saying, you don't need a bed any bigger, it just has to fit one person."

She held her hand up to stop him. "Will you just shush? If I'm going to do all the work to put this together the least you could do is be quiet and go make me food."

"You got it."

Sebastian got up from the cross-legged position he'd been sitting in, his back protesting the movement, and groaned. A snicker escaped Annabelle's lips and he ignored it, heading to the kitchen. Standing in front of the now-open fridge, he wondered what one served to their arch enemy. Too little and she'd accuse him of trying to starve her and too much she'd be looking for poison. He settled on scrambled eggs and sausage, and once those were cooked, he walked back to the bedroom to tell Annabelle it was ready.

He stopped in the doorway at the sight that met him. The bed frame was assembled, and Annabelle was standing in the middle of it, a triumphant grin on her face.

"Seriously, I was gone for ten minutes," he exclaimed.

"Sometimes I just need you to get out of my way and stop distracting me so I can get the real work done." She stepped over the low frame, one foot flexing as it touched the ground. He was beguiled once again by her bare feet, that something so innocuous could be so intimate. He watched as she padded across the carpet then slipped back into her heels, only moving when she called to him from the kitchen.

"Sir, where is your creamer?"

Sebastian walked over to Annabelle, coming up behind her so he could reach into the cabinet far above her head.

"Everyone in town calls me Sebastian. Well, except for Archy the postman, he calls me Mr. Locke." His chest brushed against the back of her head, and he lowered his for the third time that day, still not able to identify her scent. His movement was casual, under the guise of getting the creamer, but he felt her stiffen, apparently aware of their sudden closeness. She ducked under his arm, moving back toward her coffee cup, taking a gulp of the hot liquid and gasping.

"I don't think that's a good idea." Her eyes evaded his, and he was curious as to why.

"It's just a name."

"It's more than that." She took the offered creamer from Sebastian's hand and stirred some into her cup, blowing on the liquid to cool it down. "You're my boss. I don't think we should cross that line into familiarity."

Sebastian nodded, although he didn't understand where she was going with this. She was clearly gathering her thoughts, so he sat at the table with her and started dishing eggs onto plates then buttering toast. He pushed a plate and the jam jar over while he waited for her to continue. She spread a large dollop of jam on her toast and took a bite then licked the tiny bit that gathered on her upper lip. A jolt of arousal shot through him, and he understood now what she meant.

"Tell me about your family."

Well, that was a bucket of ice-cold water. And a nice change of subject. *Well done, Winters.*

"What do you want to know?"

She shot him a sly look over the top of her coffee mug. "What's it like growing up as a trust fund baby?"

Sebastian laughed. "I never got to spend anything from my trust fund when I was a baby. I got a lot of 'nos'."

"Be serious for once," Annabelle pressed. "I can't imagine what it would be like to never have to worry about anything."

"You don't exactly seem like you had a rough childhood," Sebastian shot back.

"No, I had a great childhood," Annabelle agreed. "My parents were present in just about everything I did."

"Are you an only child?" Sebastian asked.

"I have one brother who's eleven years older than me."

Sebastian whistled. "That's unusual."

"The word surprise about does it justice."

"You don't talk about him at all. Is he in town?"

"No, he moved to Japan to teach English years ago. We were never close, but like I said, I have no complaints. Whatever my parents decided they did wrong with Victor they did differently with me."

"Your parents still live in town, then?"

"Yes, they still have the same house—hey! I asked you about your family, don't change the subject."

"You have to know everything about me already."

"I don't," Annabelle promised. "For as high-profile as your family is, there's not a lot out there about it."

"Trust me when I say it takes a lot to keep it that way."

"So, tell me something I don't know." Annabelle finished the last bite of her eggs and laid the fork down. "Other than you obviously had cooking lessons, those were delicious."

"My family is closer than most people realize. They think my dad's just a corporate shark. He's good at what he does but he always made time for Sofia and me, and Mom wasn't like all the other country club moms. She raised us, not a nanny, and a lot of the kids didn't like us because of that."

"I thought she was a lawyer?"

"She is, she always was, but she put so much importance on being home and not having a nanny raise us that she stopped working until Sofia started grade school. She would always say that it was unusual for someone in her situation to have a law degree anyway, why not be downright eccentric and stay home with her kids?"

"Life wasn't all English boarding schools and vacation houses in the Swiss Alps, then?"

"My boarding school was in South Carolina and my parents sold their house in the Alps before I was born."

"I was joking, but wow. That's a life I couldn't imagine. Was it hard being at boarding school?"

Sebastian pondered this question. Not many people asked him about this time in his life, they assumed that was where a child of his means went. The fact that Annabelle thought to ask the question notched up his esteem of her by another degree.

"It wasn't easy. I was fourteen when I started at a new boarding school. I had gotten in with the wrong crowd and made some bad decisions."

"Sebastian Locke, the rebel?"

"More than that. Rebellion against your parents is normal. Almost getting a felony isn't."

"I don't believe that you had it in you to get a felony."

"Almost," Sebastian corrected. "I don't have it in me, but it scared the shit out of me that I'd gotten as close as I did. Dad shipped me off to boarding school, told me that if I was going to take over the company I needed to get away from the bad influences and get my head on straight. He was right." He was quiet for a moment, thinking back onto that time of his life. "My mom didn't want me to go. She'd gone back to work a few years before and blamed herself for what was happening."

"The mom guilt never ends, does it."

"Not for her it didn't."

"You did take over, so nepotism is alive and well, I see."

"You are so pessimistic, Winters. What happened for you to have such a bad attitude about life?"

"I don't have a bad attitude about life," she insisted, but he heard the unspoken *just about you* hovering in the air. He wanted to change her mind about him and thought the conversation they'd just had was taking them a step closer to a peaceful coexistence, but now he wasn't so sure.

"My dad said that if I was going to take over the company one day I'd need to work for it and prove to him that I was worthy. He wasn't going to just hand it to me on a silver platter and call it a day. My grandfather had built Locke Communications from the ground up and he wasn't going to see me raze it down."

"Okay, okay, you worked for it."

He was gratified to hear her say it, but he still felt that he had more to prove to her.

"I continued on to university then my Masters. I didn't stop when my dad said I'd done enough, I did more, far more that he expected me to do."

"I'm sorry, I didn't mean it like that." Annabelle reached out and laid her hand over his. The gesture was clearly meant as a soothing touch, but her silken palm on his skin was anything but, so he stood and started gathering the dishes.

"Trying to understand my upbringing can't be easy."

Annabelle joined him at the kitchen sink and took the rinsed dishes to load them into the dishwasher. She'd slipped her heels off again sometime during the meal and he found that as much as he liked her in heels, he enjoyed her natural height, that if she nestled into him she'd fit right in.

"You had a lot to live up to, didn't you?" Annabelle asked.

"Everyone has expectations in their lives. I'm not saying mine are so much more important than anyone else's, but it's the only thing I know."

He handed her a towel to dry off her hands, conscious that they were verging into an emotional territory and he didn't think either of them was prepared for that. She wouldn't even call him by his first name. She'd done so once, at the Fall Festival the year before when she'd pleaded for him to help her save love as she was trying to get Greyson and Prudence to admit their feelings for each other, and he'd savored the memory of that for far too long. He needed to get back to being a professional with her.

"Now, let's get back to the guest room. It's not going to finish itself."

Chapter Four

Sebastian's sleep that night was disturbed. After they'd resumed working in the bedroom, Annabelle had turned back into her usual self, full of biting wit. His relief was palpable, leaving behind the personal conversation they'd had about his childhood. Being back on neutral ground, a place where both their claims were clearly staked, was the best place for them.

Annabelle had a point about staying professional. A good point. A solid point. But that didn't stop him from picturing her on his beach, standing calf-deep in his water, breathing in the thick smell of pine trees. Of all the carnal images he could have, her relaxing with her guard down was the one that kept him awake most of the night.

Now he was tired and cranky and had to snap out of it before Sofia got there. She'd flown in early this morning to the Worchester airport and had chosen to drive to Amber Falls this time around, despite Sebastian's protestations that he could come and get her. She'd declined, stating that having her own car would be helpful so that he wouldn't have to chauffer her around. Last time she was here, Sebastian had been renting in town and she'd stayed in a local hotel so hadn't needed a car.

The cool morning air held a hint of humidity, promising that the day would be a warm one. It might rain later, but for now the breeze ruffled the corn crop across the street and his bad mood melted away. He chuckled, astounded — not for the first time — that he was sitting on the porch of a house he owned in rural Massachusetts, watching a corn crop sway in the breeze. If someone had told him a year ago, while he was sitting in his Atlanta penthouse lording over his concrete paradise, he would've laughed them out of the building. Then would tell them never to come back, lock the door and alert security for good measure. But now? He was nursing a mug of black coffee, content with his view, waiting for his sister to arrive.

He knew Sofia would've snapped him out of his mood, but he was grateful that he'd done it on his own as he watched her pull into the driveway. She squealed as she jumped out of her rented SUV and flew into his waiting arms, squeezing him in a bear hug.

"I'm so glad to see you, big brother," Sofia said as she released him.

Sebastian couldn't help but grin at her exuberance — she had the same effect with just about everyone she met. "I'm glad you're back."

They walked back to the SUV and grabbed her bags, Sofia stopping to look around the front of the property.

"You weren't lying when you said this was out of town." Her hand arced to the field across the street. "Isn't the corn supposed to be knee-high by the fourth of July?"

"That's an old saying. This is a good crop, according to the farm report—"

"I'm sorry," Sofia interrupted him. "The farm report?"

Sebastian felt the tips of his ears heat in embarrassment but shoved it down. "Yes, the farm report. I do run the newspaper, if you recall?"

"I know, I know," she placated. "I'm just shocked that you're still here, new house and all."

"The town isn't that bad. You know Locke Communications bought our first newspaper and I need to be here to make sure it turns a profit. I talked to Dad this week and he has his eye on another small paper in Washington."

Sofia lifted a hand to her forehead, shielding her eyes from the sunlight.

"And"—her voice was casual—"I don't suppose any sort of technological innovations from this century would allow you to do this from, say, anywhere else?"

They'd had this conversation before, and he couldn't see why she was starting in on him when her bags weren't even on the ground.

"Can we save the questions for later? You haven't even been inside."

"Oh, I'm just joking, Seb. Of course you need to be here to run the newspaper, I know that."

He hauled her large bag inside while she grabbed her smaller ones, and led her to the bedroom.

"This is nice!" He heard her say from the living room. Her voice got louder as she came into the bedroom. "It's the perfect size."

"I agree."

Sofia walked to the windows with white plantation shutters and took in the elevated terrain in the distance. "The whole place is pretty, Seb. I really mean that."

"Annabelle thought so, too."

Sofia turned, her eyebrows raised. "Annabelle?"

Dammit. Why would he mention her? He had no reason to. Sofia had met Annabelle once when she'd visited last, on a tour of the Bee offices, and it had turned into their usual shouting match between him and Annabelle. Sofia had been amused—Sebastian annoyed. "Winters." He cleared his throat. "Yes, she helped put the room together."

Sofia's eyebrows hadn't returned to their normal positions quite yet. "And Annabelle Winters was the only person that could do it? Have you driven away all your other friends?"

"Ha ha. It just so happens that they have lives. I was lucky that Winters doesn't. Or, I should say, you were lucky, otherwise it would've been couch city."

Her eyebrows finally parked back into their regular spots. "Did you have to admit to her that you're an abject failure at reading instructions?"

"I'm not a failure," he protested.

"You had to have," she continued as if he hadn't spoken. "I'm glad I'm not sleeping on the couch. I did enough of that when I backpacked through Europe."

Sebastian lifted her bags onto the bed and thought, not for the first time, how different his and Sofia's formative years had been.

"Yes, while I was taking over Dad's company you were traipsing through Europe with Stavros."

Sofia rolled her eyes. "I wasn't a traipse, it was a galivant. Besides, Dad didn't want me anywhere near Locke Communications."

Sebastian let this comment sit. It wasn't entirely true. Or, not true. Dad had stepped in with Sebastian when he thought his life needed direction and a helping hand from him. He'd tried to do the same with Sofia, but had been shot down at almost every turn. She'd been a free spirit, she still was, and he loved that about her. It did not, however, make for a stable resume.

"Enough about that," he insisted. "Let's continue the tour."

"What else do I need to see?"

"Here's the kitchen and the bathroom."

"That's great, but I already saw this."

Sebastian pointed to the door off the kitchen. "I'll show you the back porch."

"I saw the front porch, the back can't be all that diff—" Her voice trailed off as they went outside and she saw the lake. "Wow."

He told her the same information about the lake he'd relayed to Annabelle, and they sat in the chairs by the water, silent for a time.

"You know, I wasn't just having fun in Europe," Sofia started to explain. "I made some valuable contacts with people in the fashion world."

"Is fashion more to you than just wearing expensive clothes?" he asked.

"Of course it is." She dug into the sand and found a stone to throw into the water, a loud plop sounding when it landed. "Dad tried, he did, but I wasn't interested in communications, or radio or TV stations. I wanted to make clothes."

"Then why didn't you? Dad might've wanted you to work with him—"

"For him," she interjected.

"Okay, for him, but I don't see him denying you anything you asked."

"This isn't about him needing to deny me, he didn't understand me. For as close as we all are, Dad and I just didn't see eye to eye on this."

Sebastian sighed. "Dad can be hardheaded. Why didn't you go to Mom?"

"I did. She was the one that came up with the idea to travel Europe."

"No way."

"Oh yes. She told me not to stay at ritzy hotels, but to get to the heart of the cities I was in, that I'd see the fashion real women were wearing and not the inaccessible haute couture."

"She's a genius." Both Sofia and Sebastian had uttered this phrase about their mom more times than they could count.

"She truly is. Plus, she knew Dad would expect me to travel and wouldn't ask too many questions, so I could do my thing."

"Why isn't Mom running her own company?"

"That's not her style."

"I don't suppose it is."

"Speaking of style, are you coming home for Grandma's ninetieth birthday this fall? You missed eighty-nine with the move here, and she'd be devastated if you're not there."

"Grams still gives me crap about it. That birthday was the only one I've ever missed, and she won't let it go."

"She loves you so much, Seb."

"Whenever I stop to think about it, I find it so wonderful how close we are after the different turns our lives took."

"It's always been like that. Most families like ours had parents who split up, everybody doing their own thing and going their own way." She glanced sideways at Sebastian. "Even when your way took you here."

He could side eye with the best of them. "We've talked about this."

Sofia leaned forward and punched his arm. "When I was here at Christmas, you hated everything about this town. It was too cold, too remote, too small. Now you've bought a house, like you're settling down."

"The house is an investment," Sebastian explained.

"An investment in what? Your future here?"

"Maybe you should've gone to school, then I wouldn't have to explain an investment to you."

"Don't be a dolt, Seb. You know what I mean. It hasn't even been six months since I visited last and when I've talked to you since then your whole tone about this place is different. What's changed since winter?"

Sebastian's heart sped up. Did Sofia know something about Annabelle? His mind clicked. *Winter, not Winters.*

"Nothing changed," he promised. "I saw this house for sale and I thought I might as well have a nice view on a lake while I'm living in Amber Falls, so here I am."

"All right, if you say that's all there is to it, I believe you."

"What about you?" Sebastian countered. "You've been here twice. Is it just to visit your super cool older brother?"

Sofia evaded his eyes, shrugging. "Do I have to have a reason?"

"You don't, you're always welcome here. And speaking of, how long do you plan to stay this time?"

"I'm hoping two or three weeks."

Sebastian whistled. "Are you sure you're not running away from something?"

"I'm not," she assured him. "I may question your reasons for being here, but I admit there's a calmness around here that I like. And now that I have my own personal beach to lounge on in my favorite month of June, why wouldn't I stay?"

"You might be here for some of the town's Summer Solstice activities, they should start around June twentieth."

"I might. Wait, you don't know when it's starting? Isn't that kind of your job?"

"Don't start on me, too. I have to pretend to care about these celebrations enough as it is."

"Whoever else is starting in on you might have a point." She stood and brushed sand from her shorts. "I'm going to take a shower and wash the plane off me. Do we have any plans, or can I get a little rest after? My flight was early today."

"No plans, take your time."

Sebastian stayed where he was as Sofia went back inside. His mind was playing tricks on him, sure that everyone was connecting dots between him and Winters when there were no dots to connect. He couldn't hear the name of a season without thinking he was being called out for something. He needed to get a grip and he needed to get it now.

Chapter Five

Sometimes Monday morning comes at you fast. To Annabelle, seven a.m. was too damn early. She'd perfected the 'wake up thirty minutes before clock-in time and still show up absolutely polished' look. The right skirt and heels made all the difference. Throw in her trademark low bun and she presented the picture of workplace chic.

Prudence had asked if she could meet her at Books and Beans this morning before an appointment. Prudence was a popular interior designer and had a schedule so booked that she squeezed in new clients whenever she could, even if it was at the godawful crack of dawn. Never one to say no to a friend, she'd agreed. Devlin was up before the birds, a workplace hazard, and a smile lit Annabelle's face when she saw her and her employee, Emma St. Claire, behind the counter.

"Hey, guys." Annabelle walked over and slung her bag onto a chair on the way.

"What are you doing out so early?" Devlin questioned.

"And a good morning to you, too, sunshine."

"I'm always happy to see you. But for real, it's only just seven." Devlin pointed at the clock.

"You want to try the French Roast today?" Emma moved to grab a cup.

"That sounds great, thanks," Annabelle replied, taking the cup from her after it was poured.

"I'm going to work on bagging the muffins if that's okay, Devlin?" Emma moved to the display on the other end of the counter.

"That's great." Devlin leaned an elbow on the counter, her chin in her palm. "I lucked out with that one. She could run this place. So, what's up?"

Annabelle mimicked her posture. "Prudence asked me to meet her here before her appointment."

"Oh yeah, she texted me last night to make sure I'd be here this morning. I wonder what's so important?"

"Pru isn't one for theatrics so I'm guessing it's something big. She mentioned the other day that she might be leaving town with Grey."

The jangle of the front door chimed, and Annabelle straightened, turning and expecting to see Prudence. Her smile fell to the floor when Sebastian walked in. Sauntered was more like it. As if he moved in any other way.

He'd held the door open for a woman who was as beautiful as he was handsome. They were almost the same height and had the same dark hair, hers long and flowy while his was a stylish medium-length cut. She recognized her as his sister, Sofia. They'd met once after New Year's and had a good conversation, until Sebastian had picked a fight with her over her work email signature—she didn't have one and he insisted she should. It had sped downhill from there and she hadn't seen her again.

"Winters, shouldn't you be at work?" Sebastian asked, a frown on his face.

Annabelle started to reply when Sofia said, "Please. The sun is barely up, Sebastian. Plus, if she should already be there, then you're late."

I like this girl. Annabelle shot her a grateful look and held out her hand. "It's good to see you again, Sofia."

Sofia pulled her into a hug. "What can I say, I'm a hugger. I was hoping to see you again the last time I was here, but Sebastian always made excuses about you being too busy."

"I'm never too busy for someone that can put this arrogant man in his place."

"I knew we'd get along just fine." Sofia winked at Annabelle.

Annabelle turned to Devlin, ignoring Sebastian. "Dev, this is Sofia. Sofia, my good friend Devlin. She owns this coffee shop."

"How wonderful!" Sofia exclaimed. "Sebastian brought us coffee from here many times this winter when I visited, and I loved every one I tried."

"That's kind of you to say." Devlin nodded to the menu. "Anything look good this morning?"

"The hazelnut latte, please. Can I get it iced?"

"You got it."

The sound of a throat clearing broke into their conversation, and all three ladies turned to stare. Sebastian was standing behind them, hands in the pockets of his pressed dress pants, annoyance clear on his face.

"I'm sorry." Devlin motioned for Sebastian to join them. "What would you like?"

"A black coffee is fine, thanks," he answered.

Devlin poured the steaming beverage into a mug and handed it to Sebastian. "You need anything else?" At the shakes of their heads, she nodded. "Okay, I'll be back, I need to make a call."

Annabelle stared at Sebastian as if he'd sprouted two heads. She'd be less surprised if he had than at the order he'd just placed. "Black coffee?"

"What can I say, I'm a simple guy."

A snort shot out of Annabelle's nose before she could stop it. "The last coffee you had me get had ten ingredients and took just as many minutes to make."

Sebastian reached out and nudged her, clearly attempting to be playful. "Coffee orders like that keep you out of the office for longer."

Annabelle flicked her eyes down to where his elbow had connected with her arm, then back up to him. "Don't touch me, sir."

Sofia was turning red, apparently trying to hold in a laugh. She grabbed Sebastian and dragged him toward a local craft display. "Come on, brother, let's do some shopping."

Annabelle watched as Sofia showed Sebastian something from the shelf and he laughed along with her. *Interesting.* Sebastian was stoic, his smiles were rare and he was always irritable, but the couple of times she'd seen him around his sister, a different person emerged. Frankly, she wanted nothing to do with either of his personalities. That was too complicated.

She checked her watch. Seven-fifteen. The punctual-to-a-fault Prudence was late, but as if conjured up,

Prudence burst through the door with Greyson close behind.

"I'm sorry, I know I'm late," Prudence said by way of a greeting.

"I'm not sorry." Greyson pulled Prudence close and kissed her cheek. "We had the best reason for being late."

"I can guess, Grey, no need to go into details," Annabelle pleaded.

"He won't. We've talked about his oversharing," Prudence confided.

Annabelle waved over Devlin, who'd just come back out from her office and greeted the two newcomers. "I know you have a meeting soon, what's up?"

"Well." Prudence looked between the two. "You know our wedding is at the end of the summer? And the Passel Awards were moved to a few weeks from now?"

Greyson had been nominated for a Passel Award for an indie movie he'd starred in before retiring. A writers' strike had postponed the show until later this month.

She continued when Annabelle and Devlin nodded. "I told you I might have to be out of town soon, AB, and now I know I do. The issue is that the trip is the only time we could book a lot of our wedding planning appointments, and I can't cancel them and keep the same wedding date in August. Can you guys please take these over? I trust whatever you do."

Devlin groaned. "Sorry, Pru, but Gabe and I are leaving for Boston on Friday and we'll be there for at least a few weeks. We weren't planning to go but my cousin—the one I like—is having a baby and I promised her that I'd be there to help. Gabe is coming with for moral support to deal with the rest of my family." Devlin looked away as she saw Emma wave from the counter. "Shoot, Emma needs me." Devlin excused herself to go help at the front.

Prudence turned to Annabelle. "Please," she pleaded, "tell me you'll be here?"

"I'll be here," Annabelle confirmed.

"Oh, thank God! Sebastian already agreed to help as well."

"Excuse me? He already knows?" Annabelle's blood pressure shot through the roof. "I didn't agree to working with him."

"Yes, he knows. That's why he asked you to help him with his house. Grey had told him we'd probably be gone already, but we weren't. Plus, we need a guy's perspective on all this. I told Grey that this wouldn't turn into a feminine spectacle, so I need his help, too."

"It's true," Greyson interjected. "I'm all for a show, but even I know that people tend to go overboard at weddings."

Annabelle didn't hear what Greyson had said. "Absolutely not. I won't subject myself to being in his company for any longer than what I'm getting contractually paid for."

"AB, please!" Prudence pleaded.

Annabelle had just gotten done thinking about how if a friend asks for help you help them, and she couldn't go back on that now. Even if it meant working with that odious man. "Oh, all right. How bad can it be?" she asked, while shooting daggers at Sebastian across the room. He startled as if he'd been hit by one then grinned, apparently at the look on Annabelle's face. "It'll be bad, but I'll do this for you two. Just promise me that you'll have bail money set aside in case I have to murder him."

"Don't be dramatic. No one *has* to murder someone." Prudence appeared confident in this statement.

"I'm sorry, do you want me to do this?"

"Yes! I'll have bail money available for you." Prudence's confidence faltered. "Out of curiosity, what do you think would lead to a jailable offense?"

Annabelle pondered this. "Let's be honest. He could just look at me the wrong way."

"He's not that bad," Greyson offered. "Maybe spending this time together outside of work will be good for you. Show you that he might not be just the guy you see at the office every day."

Annabelle started ticking off things on her fingers. "Getting a full body massage is good for you. Getting your teeth cleaned is good for you. Getting your yearly physical is good for you. Hell, getting kidnapped by a serial killer is better for you than being forced into his company for an extended period of time over multiple days."

Greyson waved over the Locke siblings as he spoke. "You might be exaggerating, just a little bit?"

"I don't exaggerate," Annabelle deadpanned.

"She's in," Greyson told Sebastian when they reached the group.

"I was kind of hoping she'd say no."

Annabelle swiveled her head. "You already knew about this?"

"Yeah," Sebastian confirmed. "Grey asked me last week when he thought he might end up being gone."

Annabelle frowned, surprised that she was hurt by this.

"Thank you both so much, I don't know what we'd do without you." Prudence hugged each of them in turn. "The first appointment is in two days, but that's when we leave for Los Angeles. It's for my dress alterations. I'm going to give you the measurements, AB, so you can go over them with the seamstress in person."

"I should be able to handle that."

"If you want to, you can pick out bridesmaids dresses also?" Prudence offered.

"That's a great time to do it. Since Devlin isn't leaving until late Friday, she should be there as well," Annabelle speculated.

"Can I skip that one?" Sebastian asked. "I know nothing about dresses, least of all wedding dresses. Although, watching Winters try on unflattering puce dresses wouldn't be a bad way to waste an afternoon."

"That's fine," Prudence agreed. "And the dresses won't be puce."

Annabelle breathed a sigh of relief, although she knew Prudence's impeccable taste wouldn't allow her to choose anything horrid.

"What color?" She noticed the line at the counter wasn't getting any shorter, and while she wanted Devlin over here for this conversation, she'd have to have it alone.

"I don't care what color you pick."

"Wait, what?" Annabelle didn't believe what Prudence was saying.

"I mean it," Prudence insisted. "As long as the dress isn't white, it's dealer's choice."

"But you're the dealer, Pru. You hold all the cards and can even deal from the bottom of the deck if you want."

"She's serious," Greyson confirmed. "We've talked about this ad nauseam and as long as you match, she doesn't care."

"I hear puce is a great color for weddings," Sebastian joked.

Annabelle glanced to the heavens for strength.

"But hey," Sebastian put his arm around Sofia's shoulder. "I bet Sofia would love to go."

Annabelle lasered her gaze in on Sebastian. She raised one eyebrow at him and shook her head with the slightest movement. He quirked one corner of his mouth at her and nodded once. *Hm. He's going to play it like that.* She widened her eyes and stared holes into his retinas. Seriously. His eyes narrowed and his lips pursed. *Damn.*

Annabelle turned to Sofia. "Would you please come with us to get Pru's wedding dress, and offer your opinion on bridesmaid's dresses?"

Sofia smiled brightly. "I'd love to."

Prudence clapped and stood. "You guys have taken a huge weight off my shoulders, and I don't know how I'll repay you, but I'll find a way, I promise you."

"You don't have to, Pru. The fact that you're willing to front me bail money says it all."

Alarm crossed Sebastian's face. "Bail money? What would you need bail money for?"

Prudence gathered her purse and patted Sebastian's shoulder.

"Don't you worry about a thing. She's all talk." She waved at Devlin, who still had a line of customers to serve, then addressed Annabelle once again as she and Grey walked out the door. "I'll see you tonight for ladies' night?"

"Come on over at the normal time," Annabelle confirmed. She waited as Prudence not so furtively moved her eyes to Sofia before the door closed. Annabelle nodded, accepting that now her new skill was silent conversation. It *would* be rude not to invite her after her clear hesitation about wedding dress shopping.

She turned to Sofia. "I'm getting together with Devlin and Prudence tonight around seven at my place, would you like to come over also?"

"Don't do it, Sofia," Sebastian warned. "I smell the telltale signs of a trap."

"Really, sir? What kind of trap do you think I'd be inviting your sister to? While you're sitting here?"

"I don't know, Winters. Who knows what you do after working hours. You could knit or something, and be luring Sofia into learning spinsterish hobbies."

"Spinsterish is not a word," Annabelle accused.

"Look it up. Your picture is under the definition."

She rolled her eyes. "That's mature."

Sebastian took one of Sofia's hands. "Under no conditions are you to take any oaths to enter into the spinsterhood of the traveling crochet hooks. Resist everything they teach you, dear sister."

A laugh bubbled out of Annabelle at this last statement. He had a sense of humor that tickled her funny bone. How inconvenient.

Chapter Six

"That's enough," Sebastian demanded.

"Boss, I was just showing her the lines on her palm," Peter explained. "It's fascinating stuff."

"Unless you're going to put on a scarf and pull out a crystal ball, we're done here." Sebastian tried to move Sofia forward, but she wouldn't budge.

"Thank you, Peter." Sofia squeezed Peter's hand and held on a little too long for Sebastian's liking.

Sofia and Peter had gotten chummy when they'd met at Finnegan's on New Year's Eve, and, in true big brother fashion, he did not like it one bit. He'd hated it enough when she'd run off with Stavros a few years ago, but now that he could prevent someone from hitting on his baby sister, he was going to take that opportunity.

They hadn't even made it past the front desk, though, and he stood off to the side while Sofia asked the receptionist about her health. He never spent any time down here, too busy and moving too quick to notice much about the space. The waiting area was large, with couches and chairs close to the front desk.

"Now that school is out, we won't be as busy here," he heard the receptionist say.

"Why not?" Sofia questioned.

Why does it make a difference?

They both swiveled their heads to look at him.

"Did I say that out loud?" He wasn't sure if he had.

"Do you have so much going on up there that you can't even tell when you're speaking?"

Now it was his turn to swivel his head. *Of course it would be her.*

"Yes, it's me," Annabelle confirmed, just coming in through the front doors.

Did he say *that* out loud? She was driving him crazy. Like a true predator, she stalked over to them, her heels tapping on the marble floor.

"And yes, it does make a difference. If you want this newspaper to continue making a profit, it damn well makes a difference. We're the largest print paper around for hundreds of miles and schools love to bring their kids here to tour the place. We've had a few tours a month since you've been here and you haven't participated in one. If the kids have a connection to the paper, so will their parents, and we'll keep them as subscribers — or maybe even gain some."

She took a deep breath after her rant and he could see her silently counting to ten before turning to the receptionist, smiling.

"Thank you for pointing out the importance of the community having a stake in this paper staying open." She glanced back to Sebastian. "This is Mrs. Johnson, by the way, and she's worked for the Bee for thirty years." Nodding a hello to Sofia, Annabelle went to the stairwell and ascended them, apparently too busy or too annoyed to wait for the elevator.

Both pairs of eyes turned back to him.

"Of course I know your name," he assured the receptionist, hoping she wouldn't ask him what her first name was.

"If you have any other questions, please do let me know, Ms. Locke." Mrs. Johnson ignored him and waved to Sofia before picking up the ringing phone.

"Do you know her name?" Sofia stabbed the up button on the keypad once they stopped in front of the elevator.

"I said I did," his terse voice slipped out.

"Okay, I was just asking."

They stepped onto the elevator in silence.

"But Annabelle had a point," Sofia continued.

"Really, Sofia?"

"Well, she did! This isn't corporate America. These are small-town people who love their lives. It wouldn't hurt to try to understand that. You might make a difference here if you do."

The elevator dinged at their floor as if punctuating her stance, and they walked onto the floor of a bustling newspaper. For a town as small as Amber Falls, the Bee was one of the things that truly worked. They'd outperformed in all markets, which was one of the reasons it had been on Locke Communications' short list for newspapers to acquire and why they'd gone with it, and not Washington, after their final analysis.

"You should rethink joining the family business. I bet Dad could find you some outreach position, or PR job."

"No, I don't have any qualifications for something like that."

"I'm just saying, you're more intuitive than you let on."

They spent a good portion of the morning walking around the office and talking to each department. Sofia remembered most of the staff and they remembered her. He did have to admit she was good at talking with everyone, remembering what they'd spoken of in January and following up on their conversations like it was yesterday.

They ended up in the break room sipping burnt office coffee.

"We've gotten a tour of the printing room, been to all the departments and I've learned what they do to keep this place running." She cocked her head at him. "So, tell me again exactly what you do?"

Sebastian guffawed. "You know what I do. Didn't we talk about it last time?"

"No, we didn't."

"I'm the glue that holds this place together. Without me it would all fall apart."

"Are you sure about that?"

"I'm very sure."

"Okay, so tell me what you're gluing together."

Sebastian leaned back in his chair, his mind switching over from family mode to business mode. His favorite place.

"Everything comes through me. I need to know the strengths of each of my reporters so I can assign them stories that they'll excel at. I review and edit the stories, and on the rare occasion, rewrite them. After all that's done, I help to lay out the copy so it's ready for print."

"Do you do any writing yourself?"

"Sometimes. Not often, though, a few stories here and there, when I need to, or if I have something to say."

"And what do you do as the owner?"

Sebastian thought about it for a moment. "I can't differentiate the two right now."

"Why not?"

"We're not in crisis mode, yet. We bought this paper because it hit all the benchmarks it needed to, but that doesn't mean that there haven't been some scary months, when subscribers drop, or the online traffic isn't as high, so we have to figure out why."

"Who is we? Do you have to answer to anyone?"

Sebastian laughed. "Well, Dad for one. But yes, there's a board that meets monthly to go over numbers and talk about general business."

"I'm proud of you, Seb." Sofia patted him on the shoulder. "Dad threw you into this and instead of phoning it in, you've really learned about the newspaper business."

"I'd like to say I had no choice, but I did. I could've made this place sink and been back to Atlanta before the New Year, but Amber Falls seems to pull you in."

He raised his hands in surrender at her smirk of triumph.

"You got me. This town has gotten under my skin."

Sofia studied him and he squirmed under her scrutiny. "Just this town?"

"What are you getting at?"

She shrugged, appearing to back off whatever she was going to say.

"I'm not getting at anything."

He stood and deposited his Bee logo cup in the sink then motioned her to follow him. "Come on to my office, I've got a few things to handle before lunch."

They turned down the hall that led to his corner office and Sebastian felt like he was tiptoeing through his own building. He owned the place and he owned the newspaper, but he'd resorted to acting like he was just about to get away with a jewelry heist, if only he could get down this last hallway. He had to pass Annabelle's office on the way to his, and he didn't want to get stopped by her, not after the dressing down she'd given him earlier.

As it was, he made the critical error to hesitate with one step, and that hesitation brought him right to Annabelle's door. He intended to move on, but was drawn to the panic that crossed her face when his eyes met hers. Now intrigued, he stopped and went into her office instead. She slammed the lid down on her laptop, hard enough to rattle the picture frames on her desk.

"If I didn't know better, Winters, I'd think you were trying to hide something from me. You aren't watching porn, are you?"

A loud snicker sounded from behind him and Sofia whispered, "You are so fucking dense."

He ignored her and focused on Annabelle, who turned quite the shade of pink.

"Wouldn't you like to know," Annabelle shot back.

"No, I wouldn't." Sebastian realized he was lying about this, and his traitorous thoughts went to what would turn Annabelle Winters on. "You're at work, act professional."

"I'm leaving anyway. I just stopped to grab some things since I'm off this afternoon, if you don't remember."

"Why would I remember?"

"I submitted a PTO request last week for it."

"Oh, yes." Sebastian coughed.

Earlier this year, Sebastian had started making Annabelle submit Paid Time Off requests whenever she wanted time off. The company had no policy about this, no rule or system, but he'd printed off fake request forms and deposited them into her mailbox one day. Since then, she'd been dutifully filling them out. Like most things that happened with Annabelle, he didn't know why he did it, but the amusement he got when putting her unread requests in the garbage was worth it.

"You did get my request, right?"

Behind him, Sofia sighed and he heard her walk off down the hall.

"There's no such thing as a PTO request, Winters."

Annabelle, who had been putting her laptop in a bag, stopped and raised her head.

"What did you say?" Her voice was low and dangerous, almost a growl.

They'd been here before, when Sebastian questioned if he'd taken his goading of Annabelle one step too far, one tiny step at the edge where the ground would erode. So far the ground had stayed solid under his feet, but his luck might be running out. He just didn't know when to stop.

"It started as a joke," he tried to explain.

Annabelle moved toward him, her steps slow and purposeful. He swallowed with unease but willed himself not to take a step back.

"You were so annoying when you wanted to go to the cabin this winter. You didn't think I'd been invited and—" He paused.

She was right in front of him now.

"And what?" she breathed.

He ran a hand through his hair, the motion somehow bringing them closer together.

"And I don't know. It seemed funny at the time, and you kept filling out the forms so there was no reason to tell you I'd made it all up."

Annabelle poked her finger into his chest, her mouth set in a disapproving line.

"You're saying you threw out every one of my requests for five months?"

He wouldn't back away. She was close enough to brush against his chest, her heels bringing her to his chin level, and with her head tilted toward him, the brush of her lips was almost a promise. His pulse quickened at the rise and fall of her chest, her breath coming out faster as he lowered his head. Waves of displeasure radiated off her, but he sensed an awareness just below the anger, one that he couldn't place, but his body reacted to it instinctually, as if it had been waiting for it to appear.

A door slammed in the distance and Annabelle blinked rapidly, acting as though she just noticed how close they were. Sebastian needed to defuse the situation — the anger and…whatever else was happening.

He cracked a small smile. "C'mon, Winters. It was a joke."

"No, it was a misuse of your power. You had no reason to make me do that."

A hint of remorse washed over Sebastian, which he didn't often feel when it came to Annabelle. She gave as good as she got and they'd moved on each time one of them tried to best the other. True hurt showed on her face and a small fissure of doubt opened up in his chest.

No. He pushed it aside. This is what they did, how they interacted with one another. She was probably pissed that she hadn't thought of something this good and was playing him for a fool by acting hurt. At least that was what he told himself. It would be easier to play the part of the jester.

She'd moved away from him now and had gathered the rest of her belongings, bumping against him as she walked out of the office. He should let her go, cool off and be back to normal tomorrow, but that wasn't how any of this worked. He was pulled along behind her like a toy on a string, stopping when they reached the elevators.

"You can officially stop submitting requests, Winters."

She rolled her eyes and stepped into the elevator. "Ya think?"

He stopped the door from closing.

"Hey. Be nice to Sofia tonight. I know she comes off as happy go lucky, but I can tell she's going through something that she won't tell me about."

Annabelle didn't answer for a moment, then flicked his hand away so the doors could slide closed.

"I'll be as nice to her as you are to me," Annabelle finally said.

Oh crap.

Chapter Seven

Annabelle was full of shit. No matter how infuriating Sebastian was, she could never bring herself to take it out on Sofia. The interactions they'd had were good and it wouldn't be fair to Sofia to blame her for her brother's boorishness. If they were going to go bridesmaid dress shopping tomorrow, tonight was a great opportunity to get to know her more.

Sometime over the last few years, it had been decided by silent agreement that Annabelle's would be the official ladies' night hangout. Located on the top floor of one of the newer downtown condos, it boasted a large, open concept space with minimalist decorations. Annabelle didn't like clutter. A clean space meant a clear mind.

She sat back on her sofa, having finished her quick microwave meal, and nursed a glass of red wine. She'd taken a shot of tequila when she got home, trying to forget what it felt like to have Sebastian's lips so close to hers that if she closed her eyes and imagined it, she could almost feel the soft pressure of them on hers. She pressed her knees together and willed the flash of arousal that rushed through her to subside.

Anger rose through her again, an effective way to douse the need that tried to break free to the surface. That was how her afternoon had gone. Anger and lust rolling around, one after the other, sometimes at the same time, causing an uncomfortable sensation she didn't want to identify.

A knock at the door startled her out of her musings and she glanced at the clock on the wall. Only six-thirty, and the ladies weren't coming over until around seven. Curious, she looked through the peephole. Sofia. She stifled a sigh as she pulled the door open, plastering on what she hoped was a welcoming smile.

"Hi, Sofia, come in."

Sofia gave her a sheepish smile and ducked in the door. "I hope a bottle of wine will make up for Sebastian forcing me into your company for the next few days. Sins of the brother, and all that."

Remorse struck Annabelle as she took the bottle. "No, it's not forced. I'm glad you're here." Annabelle was relieved to find that the words she spoke were true as she walked over to the island and picked up a glass, tilting it to Sofia in an offer.

"I'd love some, thank you." Sofia took a seat at the island as Annabelle poured a glass out and topped hers up. "I like your apartment. I don't think of the ultramodern style when you think of a small town like Amber Falls, but you pull it off well."

"That means a lot considering you've probably traveled the world."

"Most of the world," Sofia confirmed. "At least three-quarters of it."

"I wouldn't say I'm untraveled, but I can't claim to have seen as much of it as you."

"It wasn't all by choice."

Annabelle raised her eyebrows at the cryptic words. "Were you kidnapped and taken on an around-the-world-in-eighty-days trip against your will?"

Sofia laughed, shaking her head. "I like your sense of humor, Annabelle. No, I went on a semester abroad in my senior year. But, I didn't want to go, I had a boyfriend at the time — I thought if I left it would be the end of us."

"Was it?"

"It sure was. I was smart enough to realize that if he would cheat on you while you lived in the same town, distance wouldn't promote fidelity."

"Ouch."

"I got the better end of the deal. He ended up committing fraud and going to jail."

"I would say that's one hundred percent the better end of the deal."

"Living in Europe is so different from the States. One quick plane ride and you're in another country. I took advantage of that and went everywhere I could, sometimes with classmates but mostly by myself."

Annabelle felt a pang of sympathy for Sofia, but she wasn't sure of the source of it. From the outside she'd had an enchanted life, but there was something in the way she spoke of her experiences that had a melancholy tone to it, and she wanted to know more about her, more than just because she was Sebastian's sister, but because she was her own person who had her own story to tell.

"What did you do on those trips?"

Sofia reached her arms above her head and stretched. "I tried to hit the fashion districts in each city, to get an idea of what was popular in each region. I was amazed at how different each country was, and I wanted to figure them out."

"Fashion, huh? I don't suppose your dad or Sebastian were happy with your interest in that."

"That's putting it lightly." She imitated what Annabelle guessed was Sofia's dad's voice. "'Locke's is known for one thing, and fashion isn't it.'" Her voice changed to a lower rumble. "'Get your head in the game, Sof. You've been handed this opportunity, and you need to take it.'"

"That second one sounds just like your brother."

"Dad and brother, respectively." Sofia gave a little shimmy, as if shaking off her recollection. "Enough about them. And me! Can I get a tour?"

According to the clock on the wall, they still had time before the other ladies showed up. "Sure. There's not much more to it, but let's go."

She made quick work of the place, ending up in the large master bedroom.

"This is what sold me on this particular condo." Annabelle guided Sofia through the bathroom to another room, the door hidden behind a floor to ceiling shelf. The closet was a walk in, almost as large as a typical bedroom, with two windows along the one wall that faced outside.

"Annabelle Winters. You said there wasn't much more to the place, but you were holding out on me," Sofia accused as she walked around and sorted through rack after rack of designer clothes, ending at the wall dedicated to Annabelle's preferred skyscraper heels. "How could you downplay all this, especially after I told you about loving fashion? You have some of the best brands in the world in here."

Annabelle quirked a smile. "I wanted to surprise you."

"You accomplished that!"

Sofia wandered around the room again, asking questions about specific looks or outfits.

"This all reminds me so much of Sebastian."

Annabelle choked on the sip of wine she'd just swallowed. "You take that back!"

"Not in a bad way," Sofia insisted.

"The only comparison to your brother is a bad comparison."

"He likes clean lines and the modern aesthetic also, and his closet isn't as impressive as yours, but it has just as many designer clothes in it."

Annabelle rolled her eyes. "He would, that infernal man." She darted her eyes to Sofia. "No offense."

"None taken."

Annabelle's reply was cut off when she heard the front door open and Prudence called out from the living room. As they walked out of the room, a warmth spread through her. A kinship had formed with Sofia in the short time they were together, and she found herself glad that Sofia was there, despite who her brother was. Sofia fit in well with the rest of the group. Devlin and Prudence warmed to her, although she'd had no doubts that they would.

Their conversation flowed as if they'd all been friends forever, until Prudence brought up the one thing Annabelle didn't want to talk about. Atlanta.

"Atlanta?" Sofia questioned. "You lived in Atlanta?"

Prudence darted a glance to Annabelle, her gaze apologetic, before answering. "After college AB and I moved there."

"What a small world. That's where Sebastian and I grew up. Where did you work?"

Devlin now got in on the glancing.

"I'm missing something," Sofia stated.

Prudence jumped in to take the heat. "I worked with Aiden McCall Designs. Every day was a learning experience."

Sofia whistled. "That's impressive, Aiden McCall decorated my parents' last house, and if you have a fraction of his aesthetics, Amber Falls is lucky to have you here."

"We are lucky." Devlin clinked Prudence's glass. "She's been helping me with the new space in my shop and I swear that half of the people come in just to see how she designed it."

"That's not true, Dev," Prudence insisted. "Your place could be bare but for the tables and chairs and it would still be full every day with people wanting your coffee and treats."

"That's kind of you to say." Devlin smiled.

"I worked on some of the Locke Communications remodeling when Annabelle was there."

Annabelle groaned.

Sofia set her glass down on the table with a clank. "What? You worked for my brother in Atlanta, too?"

"Well, not directly."

"I knew there was something weird between you two," Sofia crowed.

"Weird doesn't begin to explain it." Prudence moved out of the way as Annabelle took a swipe at her.

"Tell me more." Sofia moved over to sit next to Annabelle. "I need to know everything."

With a tequila shot and three glasses of wine in her, Annabelle recited her history with Sebastian.

"I wrote a novel." Annabelle figured it would be easier to just get it all out. "I thought it had promise and a friend offered to set up a meeting with Locke Communications."

"That sounds standard."

"I thought so, until I met with Sebastian. He acted surprised that I was in his office then he paged through the manuscript and ripped me to shreds."

"Oh, Annabelle, that's terrible." Sofia laid her hand over Annabelle's.

"It wasn't until later that that I started working there, but I avoided him like the plague after. In fact, I don't think he ever knew I was an intern." Annabelle shrugged with an indifference she didn't feel. "It happened, and it was over years ago."

"I hate to play devil's advocate." Sofia grimaced. "But you met in person with Sebastian?"

"Yes."

"That part is what's throwing me off. He's the CEO, he doesn't take meetings with unpublished authors— there's an entire imprint with employees that would do that."

"I thought it seemed strange, too. It wasn't until I was in his office that what I was doing hit me, and by then it was too late. I just had to stand there and take his censure."

"Regardless, that doesn't excuse him for however he treated you," Sofia insisted. She took a long drink from her wine glass. "When did you say this happened?"

"Oh gosh." Annabelle pretended to think about it when it was ingrained in her psyche. "I think it happened in May, about five years ago?"

"Yep," Prudence jumped in. "That sounds about right."

Sofia sighed. "Once again, I am not excusing his behavior whatsoever, but that's when he broke up with Serena."

A white-hot poker of jealousy shot through Annabelle. For a woman. That her boss, who she hated, broke up with years ago. *What is happening to me?*

"Who?" she choked out.

"Serena Wallace."

"Of the Atlanta Wallaces?" Prudence asked.

"The very same." Sofia nodded. "They went out for years and he was serious about her. From what I got out of him with my needling questions after it happened, he'd asked her to marry him, and she shot him down like they'd just been acquaintances and not a couple for years."

"Oh no." Devlin's hand went to her heart, like she was pained to hear the story.

"That's not all." Sofia set her glass down. "It sounded like she told him she was cheating on him, too. I only remember the date because he proposed on May Day."

Annabelle's vision tunneled and she flashed back to the day she'd first met him in his office. May the second. A day after he had his heart broken.

She'd taken the elevator up to the executive floor, curious riders taking stock of her as they got off on lower floors and she didn't. Most people didn't ride up to the top of the building, but she had an appointment. Her friend, Brian, had set it up, insisting that Sebastian Locke would love to meet with her, and he couldn't wait to hear her pitch.

She walked down the hallway, her confident steps faltering only when she reached his assistant's desk.

"Annabelle Winters to see Sebastian Locke."

The curly haired assistant, who couldn't have been a day over twenty, looked down his nose at her, a feat made even more impressive that he was sitting down.

"Is Mr. Locke expecting you?"

Doubt washed over her once again. She'd known Brian for only a few weeks, so calling him 'friend' was a bit of a stretch, especially after she'd turned him down when he'd asked her out.

"Yes. Brian Smith set an appointment up for me."

At this the door opened and a small, balding man in an ill-fitting suit scurried out, clutching a legal pad to his chest. He ran a hand over his face and muttered, "Good luck."

She'd taken this as her queue and entered the office, cutting off the assistant's squeak as she closed the door.

There he was, at his desk. The first thought that ran through her head was that she'd never seen anyone so attractive. The sleeves of his white dress shirt were rolled to the elbow and the top few buttons were undone. His olive skin glowed.

"What now, Stevens?" he barked.

Annabelle didn't know what to say. He was expecting someone else, maybe his assistant.

When he didn't get an answer he looked up. "You're not Stevens."

"Clearly."

His eyes narrowed. Wrong answer.

"Who the hell are you?"

"Annabelle Winters. Our mutual friend, Brian Smith, said you'd meet with me about my novel." She held out her

hand, her book clutched in it, grateful she'd thought to bring an extra copy.

She thought that he wasn't going to say anything until he motioned her forward with a wave. To her eternal chagrin, she stumbled on her heels as she walked to his desk, laying her manuscript down. Then, he proceeded to ignore her.

She waited for one, then two minutes while he typed away on his laptop, clearing her throat when it dragged on into three. He took her manuscript, paging through it. She'd sent over a copy a week ago in preparation for this meeting, so she assumed he was reacquainting himself with her work. She wasn't prepared when no more than thirty seconds later he tossed it back on the desk.

"Your prose is mediocre, and your choice of adverbs is execrable."

She was stunned. This was not what she was expecting.

"The plot is trite and derivative of Frances Shanty, but it's not a single percent as good as hers."

Annabelle didn't know what to do. She stood there, her mouth open, trying to process the words he'd just spoken. He destroyed her novel, the one she'd spent years working on. In a matter of seconds, her cautious optimism crashed into devastation.

"Are you expecting me to say anything else?" Sebastian's eyes and voice were cold.

"Bastard," the whisper escaped her lips. So unprofessional. So true.

His mouth tipped up in a sardonic smile. "Yes. Yes I am."

She floated back into herself, her palms slick with sweat and her heart pounding at the memory, like she'd just walked out of his office.

"So, we'll just let AB marinate for a bit," she heard Prudence say.

Annabelle shook her head, the haze of her memory fading away. "No, I'm here."

"I hope so." Devlin's eyes were full of concern. "You were gone for a while."

"I saw him the day after Serena broke up with him." She looked at Sofia. "No wonder he had a bad reaction to my romance novel."

She felt a glimmer of pity for him. It sounded like Serena had hit him with one of the worst kinds of betrayal, and no matter how important or rich or handsome he was, the fact remained that he was human, and having to perform at his level on a good day had to be hard, but on a bad day? On a cataclysmic day? He couldn't just stay home and eat ice cream by the gallon while listening to sad songs and crying into a box of tissues. He had a company to run, people that depended on him.

Maybe the time had come to let him off the hook, to slacken her line in him just the slightest. Since Locke Communications had bought the Bee, she'd been infuriated with him, angry that he'd now invaded her personal space. She hadn't granted him a trial period — he'd been on probation the second she caught wind of him in Amber Falls. She'd never sabotaged him, she wasn't that petty and she loved the paper too much, but she sure hadn't helped him to succeed.

Annabelle took in the group of women sitting with her, all of them silent and patient, waiting for her to continue.

"I'm sorry to hear about what happened to him." Annabelle turned to Prudence. "Maybe we'll get along more when we go to the wedding planning appointments together, Pru."

"I have no doubt you will," Prudence said. "I wouldn't have asked you both if I thought you would fight the whole time."

"I won't be there as a buffer," Devlin told her, "and I'm sorry for that."

"That's okay. I've dealt with that arrogant ass enough that I know how to handle him." She turned to Sofia. "No offense."

"You can stop saying that. I grew up with the guy, I know what he can be like," Sofia confided.

"Speaking of asses," Devlin segued, "not arrogant ones, but nice ones. When is Wyatt Reed coming into town?"

"I thought you guys knew?" Prudence looked around at the ladies. "He got in last night."

"What!" Devlin and Annabelle shrieked in unison, Annabelle relieved at the change in subject.

"Wyatt Reed is in Amber Falls?" Sofia looked confused. "This must be the strangest small town to ever exist."

"When Grey retired from acting and decided to move here, one of the reasons was because the university offered him a teaching position. That includes running the summer stock production every year," Prudence explained. "The writers' strike pushed the Passel Awards off until next week when summer stock starts, and Grey asked Wyatt to fill in."

"But I thought they didn't get along?" Sofia's confusion deepened. "Everything in the tabloids makes it sound like they have a major feud between them. Like, major. *Person* magazine had an entire issue devoted to it."

"I had the same questions when I first got here." Devlin refilled wine glasses as she spoke. "I guess there was never a feud, right, Pru?"

"No, almost everything printed in those magazines was made up. It's true that Wyatt and Grey were friends that took different paths, but neither of them ever faulted the other for their choices. Although," Prudence confided, "Grey couldn't stand it when he was vilified for being a single Hollywood actor and they let Wyatt move on from all that. When they dubbed him 'Saint Wyatt', I thought Grey was going to explode."

"Yeah, I remember that." Sofia nodded. "Wyatt did do a complete one-eighty, though. One week he was bedding every beauty there was and the next week he was starring in indie movies and dedicating his life to charity and volunteering."

Annabelle looked thoughtful. "I wouldn't say dedicating..."

"I'm not denying that he changed," Prudence agreed. "Something must've happened to him because he's much quieter now. He was in those *Tombs of Egypt* movies and he was a lot like the character he played, loud and outgoing, but it's like his volume button was turned down. He doesn't like the spotlight anymore and keeps to himself. In fact, they wanted him to present at the awards and he declined."

"This is a great place for that." Devlin turned to Sofia. "Amber Falls will let him be."

They were all quiet for a few moments until Prudence spoke. "We're taking a private plane this time."

"I didn't know Grey had that much money," Annabelle teased.

"Oh yeah, he's private chef rich." Prudence winked.

"Private chef rich?" Sofia sighed. "If I could aspire to only one thing, it's to being private chef rich."

Damn, she was really beginning to like her. She tilted her head at Sofia. "You have to be, too."

"My parents are."

"Isn't that the same?" Devlin asked.

"Not in our family. If I needed the money, I know I could ask Dad and I'd get it, but we Lockes prefer to make it on our own. Grandpa Locke started it all and we're just following suit. I've made my own money, despite my dad's doubts."

"Hell yeah, you have." Prudence raised a glass for a toast. "Here's to unbeatable and unbreakable ladies." A loud buzz sounded from the coffee table and Prudence picked up her phone. "Speak of the devils. Grey said they're all down at Finnegan's right now. Should we go crash guys' night?"

"Wyatt included?" A gleam flashed in Sofia's eyes. "I've never heard of a better idea."

"You're not as excited to meet Grey?" Prudence looked crestfallen.

"It's different when they're in love in real life," Sofia explained. "Grey is off limits and Wyatt isn't."

Annabelle's stomach clenched at the thought of seeing Sebastian outside of their normal work setting. Every time she did, it seemed like she let her guard down and he trounced her somehow. But, she wasn't going to become a shrinking violet because of him. Unbeatable and unbreakable ladies never cowered.

Chapter Eight

The hair on the back of Sebastian's neck stood up. Something wasn't right, and his body was responding to certain doom. He glanced around at the other men gathered at the table and they all seemed at ease, without a care in the world. Gooseflesh prickled on his arms and a shiver ran through his body. There was a reason he was reacting like this, and he knew he'd find out soon. *Something wicked this way comes.*

The door to the bar jangled open and he swiveled in his chair, on high alert. He saw his sister first. His sister who should be at Annabelle Winters' place, not walking into Finnegan's bar. She laughed and held the door open for The Reason. The reason he didn't sleep last night. The reason he tossed and turned, still feeling the slight pressure of her chest brushing against his, sure that it was her pebbled nipples straining against her shirt, begging to be sucked.

The only relief he'd finally gotten last night was when he'd taken himself in hand to release the pressure that had built up in him since that moment. He'd stroked himself as he replayed their last encounter. This time, instead of letting Annabelle move away, he wrapped his arms around her and crushed her to him. He would have no doubt that he'd be touching her nipples, just like she'd have no doubt that his erection was pushing against her midriff. He'd hike one of her legs up as his tongue invaded her mouth, memorizing every contour and crevice.

Instead of letting her walk away, he'd reach a hand up and cup one of her breasts, his fingers playing with the nipples that were enticing him through her shirt, his mouth absorbing the moan that she couldn't stop from escaping her at this teasing. Last night he'd stroked his cock hard and come in a blind rush of lust before he could think of them going any further. He only had to slake this need and to banish her from his mind before he imagined what her breasts would taste like, or how her hands would stroke him.

Masturbating to Annabelle was becoming a common occurrence, but it had to be done fast, for his own sanity. He never allowed himself to dwell on why he needed to picture her as he pleasured himself, or why he wouldn't let this fantasy go beyond kissing. But the kissing…in his mind the kissing was more intimate than the act of fucking.

He had a hard enough time keeping up a professional façade in the office without letting himself envision in full technicolor what it would be like to pound into Annabelle. So, he'd stroke himself off when he needed to and go to work the next day, inciting her into anger to tamp down his desires.

To say it was an inconvenience that he got as hard as concrete when Annabelle walked through the door of Finnegan's tonight would be an understatement.

Her eyes found his, like magnets drawn to one another, and bounced away just as fast, magnetic repulsion restoring the natural order of things. She looked like she always did, put together and elegant, but he found himself noticing the little things about her. The way she knotted her hair at the nape of her neck, that her dress shirts were always unbuttoned down three buttons — never two and never four. She wore a ring on the middle finger of her right hand. It wasn't fancy, but she wore it every day.

As he catalogued Annabelle's appearance, he'd missed that Gabe was talking to him.

"Did you know they'd be coming out tonight?" Gabe looked annoyed to have to ask for, apparently the second time.

"How would I know?" Sebastian spat out with more force than he'd intended. "I don't keep tabs on any of them."

"Fair point," Gabe conceded.

Sebastian felt the stare of Greyson before he saw it.

"You sure look like you're keeping tabs on someone." Greyson nodded toward Annabelle, who had stopped at the bar with the other ladies.

"You're full of shit, Greyson." Sebastian glanced at Wyatt Reed, the fourth member at their table. "She's fair game, just so you know. I have no interest in anyone in Amber Falls." He ignored the small pang in his chest at these words.

Wyatt shook his head. "I'm not here for any reason other than to help Greyson out with summer stock. This summer will be an exercise in celibacy for me. I'm not looking for a one-night stand or a summer fling, I'm just here to help.

"Oh, God, that sounds terrible." Greyson stood. "I'm gonna go see Pru, I'll be back."

"Hey." Sebastian pointed to the dartboard. "We haven't finished our game."

Greyson waved a hand in dismissal and walked off. Gabe shrugged and left as well, heading over to Devlin at the bar.

They were gathered for their Thursday night Finnegan's Gentleman's Ye Olde Dart League. No one took credit for the name, but someone had come up with it late one night after quite a few drinks. They didn't meet every Thursday, but rather when their schedules allowed. Sebastian was grateful for their dart nights even though he was the worst player by far.

Sebastian turned to Wyatt. "So, celibacy, huh?"

Wyatt Reed was a quiet man. Quieter than he'd expected. He was an action star, like Greyson, but Greyson had an exuberance about him that was hard to contain. Wyatt was reserved and always seemed like he was weighing the conversation in his head before he spoke. More than once since they'd met, Sebastian had wondered what happened to the man to make him so cautious and restrained.

"I have no interest in entanglements right now."

Sebastian elbowed him. "You don't have to get entangled with someone to have some fun."

A shadow crossed Wyatt's face and he retreated more into himself if that was possible. He glanced over at the group still at the bar and Sebastian noticed that his gaze lingered on Annabelle for longer than he was comfortable with. As far as he knew, they hadn't yet been introduced, but uncertainty bubbled inside him.

The front door's bell broke both their spells and Emma breezed through to a chorus of welcoming chatter from the bar. Within moments, the whole group meandered back to the two men and introductions were made.

"We're glad to meet you, Wyatt." Annabelle shook his hand. "When Grey said your feud was over, we were all relieved."

Wyatt rolled his eyes. "Everything was exaggerated."

"Speak for yourself," Greyson joked. "I was ready to start bribing casting agents to blacklist you."

Prudence cuffed Greyson on the arm. "You would've done no such thing."

"No, but I might've written some strongly worded reviews, anonymously of course," Greyson admitted.

"He's had so many good reviews that your campaign of destructiveness wouldn't make a dent." Annabelle smiled at Wyatt. "I loved your last movie, *The Riverbank*."

"Hey, thanks. I read the book a long time ago."

"Oh? I didn't know it was a novel." Annabelle moved closer to Wyatt.

"It was written in the nineteen thirties but never had widespread popularity. I read it over the summer in high school between my junior and senior years and it always stuck with me."

Annabelle dug her elbow into Sebastian's side and stepped in front of him, blocking him out of their conversation.

He dropped back, keeping a wary eye on the two as he moved next to Emma and Sofia.

"Hey, big bro. I was telling Annabelle earlier that this is the strangest small town I've ever been in, and Emma and I were just discussing the same thing."

"It's true." Emma leaned in. "We're standing in a bar in a town with a population of maybe twenty thousand, and there are two well-known actors a few feet away from us."

"This can't be that rare, can it?" Sebastian asked.

Emma waved her hand in dismissal. "I'm not talking about Sundance, or whatever small mountain town Hollywood decides to overrun next. This is Amber Falls."

"I guess you're right," Sebastian conceded.

"I'm being so daft." Emma clapped a hand to her forehead. "This is nothing to you two. You're Lockes. You must have more money than both Greyson and Wyatt combined."

Sofia winked at Emma. "But none of the notoriety."

"Speak for yourself, dear sister." Sebastian wagged his eyebrows. "I'm plenty notorious."

A peal of laughter distracted himself from the conversation and he focused on Annabelle and Wyatt, pretending not to watch their interactions. She was smiling at Wyatt, still. Beaming, if he was forced to choose a descriptive word. The traitorous thought crossed his mind that she never looked at him like that. They worked together day in and day out and she barely had cracked a smile for him. He could count on one hand the number of times her lips tilted to an upright position, rather than a frown.

He observed the other pairs in the room. Devlin was looking at Gabe like that. Prudence was looking at Greyson like that. And now Annabelle was looking at Wyatt like that. *Fuck.*

Sebastian excused himself from the conversation and walked to the far side of the bar, a private corner where he didn't have to watch Annabelle make moony eyes over Wyatt Reed. He was sipping his whiskey when she approached. The Reason.

She came to stand next to him, too close, their shoulders brushing, then retreating, only to brush again.

"What can I get for you and the Mrs.?" the bartender asked.

Annabelle looked comically horrified, and Sebastian felt a momentary pang that she would be so mortified at the thought of the two of them being mistaken for a couple before saying, "Her? There's no way in hell she'd ever be my Mrs. She's what you'd call a termagant, if you must know."

She kicked him on his shin.

The bartender shifted. "Ah, well, either way, do you want a drink?"

"I'll need a whiskey to put up with him for another second."

He shot a look to her. "Did you come over here to shove me out of the way again?"

"I didn't shove you." Annabelle turned around, her back to the bar top, facing him. "If anything, it was a tiny nudge so I could get closer to hear him."

"I bet you wanted to get closer." He knew he sounded salty, but the tone just came out. "Couldn't get the movie star you've known your whole life, so you might as well make a run for the next one you see?"

"Wow, really?" She narrowed her eyes at him, and even he knew he was being an ass. A light dawned in her eyes, and he took a step back from the force of her glare. "You're jealous."

"The hell, Winters? What would give you that idea?" *Just because I notice you don't laugh at my jokes or smile at me like that doesn't make me... Oh shit.*

"You're upset over me having a conversation with another man, then you accuse me of secretly wanting my best friend's fiancé." A sly smile crossed her face, slow and deliberate. "You're jealous."

"And you're certifiable." He took another step back.

Annabelle apparently wasn't going to let him retreat and came close enough that static electricity jumped from her body to his as she laid her hand on his chest. "You totally want me."

His mouth fell open as a retort died on his lips. She leaned in, her mouth inches from his, then gave him a shove.

"Get over yourself, you harebrained ninny. If you had any sense at all, you would've seen that Wyatt couldn't keep his eyes off Emma."

He replayed the scene in his head. A coy Annabelle looking at Wyatt and Wyatt looking with longing at...Emma. Even now, when he observed the rest of the group, Wyatt wasn't showing Annabelle any more interest than he was any of the other ladies. True, they were across the bar so it was hard to gauge, but maybe she was right.

"What are you doing up here?" he deflected back to her.

"You were squeezing that tumbler so hard I could see the whites of your knuckles, so I decided to see what was wrong."

Sebastian let his own sly smile bloom. "You care enough to want to know how I'm doing."

Her cheeks reddened. "I needed a drink," she explained. "You were a hazard of coming to the bar."

He gestured with his head to the emptiness of the area.

"Why do you look so mad if it's not because of Wyatt?"

Sebastian was saved from having to reply when he heard Greyson shout, "Get over here, you two."

He motioned with his hand. "After you."

"No, sir, by all means, please go ahead."

"I know you want to stare at my ass, Winters, but you're being so obvious about it."

She made a noise of annoyance and stormed off.

"You haven't won yet, can you save the speech for the Passel Awards?" Gabe was asking when they got back to the group.

"I'm not making a speech, I'm just letting you all know we're leaving tonight and won't be back until July, I think." He turned to Prudence, and she nodded in confirmation.

"July!" Devlin exclaimed. "But that's like three or four weeks."

"We're going to work on packing up Grey's house to put on the market," Prudence said.

"Don't you have people that can do that for you?" Emma asked. "Isn't the point of being rich and famous that you have 'people'"?

Greyson winked at Emma, a blush appearing on her cheeks. "If I must recount everything that happened this fall I will, just for you. I fired my agent, Nadia. And Bradford." He shot a pointed look at Wyatt. "Bradford decided he was wasting his personal assistant skills with me and went back to our very own Mr. Reed."

Wyatt cracked a small smile. "He was, and he did."

Greyson waved his hand with a melodramatic flourish. "It's all water under the bridge, dear friend."

"I should hope so. You stole him from me first, Grey," Wyatt pointed out.

"I prefer the term 'redistribution of labor'."

"You can prefer whatever term you like." Wyatt turned to Emma, and she blushed deeper. "He's better off back with me. He said Greyson was high maintenance."

Prudence let out a snort of laughter. "He's not exactly wrong, but now I get to deal with all of that."

"Prudence mentioned that you were here to help with summer stock?" Sofia moved closer to Wyatt.

"I am. I did it when I was in college and it was a great experience."

"I don't suppose you could use some help? I love working with clothes and I could do the costumes." Sofia clicked through pictures on her phone to show Wyatt and Greyson.

"That sounds great, Sofia. We'd be lucky to have you." Wyatt turned to Emma. "What about you? We could always use an extra helping hand."

"Yeah," Greyson added. "The more the merrier."

Emma's face reddened, and Sebastian thought she was a little flustered with the attention of two movie stars focused on her.

"I guess I could, but I don't know much about all that stuff."

"Don't worry, I'll help you out." Wyatt smiled at Emma.

"It seems like it's all ending up like it should," Emma said.

These words prompted Sebastian to think about fate and he darted a covert glance to Annabelle. Every decision in his life had led him to this moment. Standing here, with a group of friends he never thought he'd have. Annabelle was talking to Prudence and Devlin, her eyes glowing and her face radiating happiness. Everyone in their group looked content and carefree, and he'd been around long enough to know what a rarity that was. Jaded trust fund babies, overworked publishers and bored, golf-playing CEOs was what he was used to. This whole town was a revelation, and he wasn't sure if it was the town or the air or the people, but he was starting to think that it wasn't so bad.

Chapter Nine

"C'mon, Annabelle," Devlin pressured. "Just try it on."

"No, I won't. We're here to find bridesmaid's dresses for Pru's wedding and I won't waste your time putting on wedding dresses."

Annabelle, Devlin and Sofia were at Bridal Bliss, one of the main street storefronts. Prudence had her pick of couture dresses but ultimately decided that a local designer would suit her just fine. Prudence had tasked them with finding bridesmaid dresses while she was gone with Greyson, and Annabelle was hoping they'd find the right dresses soon and they'd be done with it. Not that a day of clothes shopping didn't appeal to her. The fact that it was for a wedding, one where she couldn't stop picturing Sebastian, was what got to her. They'd tried on a few dresses already that hadn't been right, so they were sifting through the stock one more time.

"I get it. You're embarrassed that with your impeccable style you can like something at a discount bridal shop for"—Sofia lifted the tag—"six hundred dollars?"

Annabelle had to admit, the dress was perfect even though it was nothing like what she'd imagined when she dreamed of her wedding dress. She'd pictured a modern, tea length dress. Nothing fancy, just enough to get the job done at the courthouse in a quick ceremony. When she saw this flowing off-white perfection, she'd let out a gasp and had been drawn to it. Even now, as she was arguing about trying it on, she couldn't help but touch the silken texture and the delicate beading.

"It has nothing to do with that," she insisted. "No weddings are in my future and it would be a waste of time to try it on."

Sofia raised an eyebrow. "That could change very soon."

"Unless Boston starts importing eligible bachelors to the streets of Amber Falls, I'm afraid that I'm going to stay single for now."

"Why are you so sure of that?" Sofia asked.

"Because Annabelle has no need for a man," Devlin said, as if by rote, her voice taking on a drone. "If Jane Austen could lead a full life without ever getting married, so can she."

"Jane Austen, Florence Nightingale and Susan B. Anthony, just to name a few," Annabelle added on.

"You know for sure they were happy?" Sofia pressed. "You've asked them?"

"I was just starting to like you, Sofia," Annabelle grumbled.

"And I'm liking you even more." Devlin flicked more dresses aside on the rack. "It's about time someone takes AB out of her comfort zone."

"Just because you and Pru found love doesn't mean that everyone else wants to pair up. I'm fine just as I am."

"But you don't *try*," Devlin explained.

"Why bother." Annabelle shrugged. "I'm happy now."

They shopped in silence until Annabelle heard a muffled voice from the other side.

"My brother is single."

Annabelle whipped the clothes aside, revealing Sofia.

"Your brother is also an arrogant, smug, self-absorbed jerk."

Sofia just shrugged. "So?"

"I have much better taste than that. No offense."

"She does pride herself on her taste," Devlin said from across the room.

"What does that matter when you're alone all the time?" Sofia philosophized.

"I'm not alone all the time. I've got my family and my friends."

Annabelle moved on from the rack and tamped down the gloomy emotions she'd been having of late. Her two best friends were paired off and that meant they weren't available like they'd been in the past. They still had their weekly lunches and ladies' nights, but her life seemed different. She couldn't explain what was off, and she wasn't putting any blame on Prudence or Devlin. It didn't even have anything to do with them being paired off, but she was very aware of the passage of time and the perception that she was stuck in a rut just wouldn't go away.

Annabelle was starting to notice her friend's absences, even though Devlin was still here, and Prudence had been gone for less than a day. Thinking about being without them for the short time they'd be gone made her feel like she was in less of a rut and on more of a road of potholes after a bad winter, bouncing around and being jostled until her teeth chattered.

"I can see the wheels spinning in your head."

Annabelle jumped as Devlin spoke close behind her.

"Not spinning. The wheels are going the same pace as ever."

Devlin held up a black dress, letting her off the hook. "What do you think about this one?"

Annabelle cocked her head as she studied it. "I like it. It's not too fancy and I think we could all wear it again at some point."

"I think we found it, Sofia," Devlin called.

They waited a moment as they heard Sofia but didn't see her. After some rustling Sofia appeared from around the corner with the dress that had stopped Annabelle in her tracks.

"I guessed you were a size four." Sofia walked to a dressing room and opened the door. "I'm going to put it in here. You might as well try it on, since you're going to get undressed for the bridesmaid's dress."

An attendant brought out the last bridesmaid dresses they'd chosen and handed Annabelle one of them. She ignored Sofia as they went into the changing rooms.

"If anything" — Annabelle's voice was loud enough to be heard through the door — "Devlin should be the one trying on wedding dresses."

She heard Devlin sigh. "I don't want to get ahead of myself. It's going to be hard enough spending all this time with Gabe at a wedding without it seeming like I'm pressuring him into anything. We've only been together for a few months."

"Greyson and Prudence only dated for short time before he proposed, right?" Sofia asked from the main room.

"That's true," Devlin confirmed, "but they'd known each other for decades. I don't think they have as much baggage as Gabe and I do, and I want to take it slow and not jump into anything."

"You're already living together," Annabelle pointed out.

"That was more out of necessity. Emma needed a place to stay, and I was at Gabe's almost all the time anyway."

They opened the dressing room doors at the same time and Sofia clapped in approval.

"Those dresses are timeless and classic." Sofia moved toward them and made some minor adjustments to the fit. "You can keep trying dresses on, but I think this one is a winner."

Devlin twisted in front of the mirror. "Prudence will love these."

After the boutique's staff made notes for alterations, Sofia came up to Annabelle and whispered, "Just try it on. No one else will know."

Annabelle shut the dressing room door in reply, but as she removed her dress, her eyes kept drifting to the gown hanging on the wall. Her resolve faded, drawn once again to the simplicity of the design and the intricate bead work. She didn't realize she was reaching out to take the dress until it was off the hanger and in her hands.

Sofia was right. No one needed to know. She could be frivolous for just a few minutes — what was the harm of allowing herself to try it on? She'd tried on plenty of clothes over the years. Just because this was a wedding dress didn't make it that much different than anything else. Before she could change her mind, she pulled the dress on. For such a fanciful design, it was, overall, an uncomplicated garment.

She opened the door and stepped out. "Can I have some help with the laces?"

Devlin squealed when she saw Annabelle. "Yes!"

Sofia moved her to the front of a three-way mirror and began tightening the corset.

"I knew you'd be stunning in this."

"It doesn't make me look too short?"

"No. A mermaid style might, but there's so much volume with the train that your height is irrelevant."

"You know when you stopped in my office the other day and your brother accused me of watching porn?"

"Gross, yes I remember."

"I was looking at wedding dresses. He would've never let me live it down if he knew what I was really doing."

"All this talk about being happy just as you are was lip service, then?"

"No, not lip service. A gal can dream, right?"

"There's no harm in that," Sofia confirmed then stepped back and stood next to Devlin, allowing Annabelle to see herself in the mirror.

Annabelle couldn't move. The reflection staring back at her was of a person she didn't know. Annabelle was cool and collected. Feelings and emotions had no place in business and being a woman in a male-dominated profession had disabused her of any instinct to have emotions, let alone to show them. What she saw in the mirror now was a whimsical Annabelle. An Annabelle who would dance in the moonlight, go for a walk in the rain, and maybe even wear flats.

She twirled around, her hands floating over the dress, aware that Devlin and Sofia were watching her, but not caring. She liked this Annabelle. She was seeing who she'd been before she'd gone to Atlanta, before she'd become jaded by the business world, obsessed with bylines and deadlines.

Reality crashed over her. What the hell. A dress didn't change anything. It didn't change her situation or profession. It sure wouldn't make a difference when she'd go back to work. She was the same old Annabelle, and there weren't any eligible bachelors in Amber Falls.

"Not always the bridesmaid, are we, Winters? Or is this just wishful thinking?"

Annabelle's stomach sank at the voice behind her. *This isn't happening.* Sebastian Locke was not standing behind her in a bridal shop watching her have an existential crisis about how many different Annabelles there were.

Of all the things Sebastian could catch her doing, trying on a wedding dress was one of the worst that could happen. Her face flamed, hot and humiliated.

"Shoot, I forgot he was picking me up here for lunch." Sofia appeared sheepish but Annabelle didn't believe her for one second.

Annabelle turned, willing down the embarrassment trying to rise in her. She won the battle, having determined a long time ago that she'd win any battle that had to do with Sebastian.

"You have nothing better to do than to creep on a woman trying dresses on?" she shot back.

"Woman?" Sebastian clearly feigned confusion.

"Knock it off, Seb." Devlin walked over to Annabelle and adjusted a strap on her dress. "I have a few more minutes with AB before I leave, and I'd like it to not be filled with this weird tension between you two."

The apparent confusion on Sebastian's face turned real. "I'm just here to pick my sister up for lunch, I promise."

Devlin held up her watch. "As fun as this is, I've gotta go."

Annabelle ignored Sebastian and faced Devlin. "Why does this sound like a goodbye?" she asked.

"This isn't a goodbye, it's a see you later. We'll be back before you know it." Devlin reached out, gathered Annabelle into a hug and whispered into her ear, "Let things happen, AB. You might be surprised." Devlin pulled away and turned to Sofia. "It was nice to meet you. I hope you'll visit Amber Falls again soon."

Sofia looked between Annabelle and Sebastian. "I think I'll be back."

Devlin waved and left the store, leaving behind an awkward silence.

Annabelle fidgeted with a ruffle on the dress. "I'm going to change. We should be done for the day after this, though, if you want to take off, Sofia."

She noticed Sebastian's gaze lingering on her bust before snapping to her face. "We're not done today. It's Friday and you still have a job to do."

"C'mon, Seb, it's Friday at *noon*. Just let her have the rest of the day off," Sofia insisted.

Sebastian shook his head. "Sorry, but I've got a business to run, and I need her."

Sofia gave him a pointed glare.

"There," he corrected. "I need her there. Tell you what. I'll buy you both lunch, then Winters and I can head back to work."

Annabelle couldn't think of a less desirable thing than to go to lunch with Sebastian after he'd watched her twirl around in a wedding dress like she was a little girl.

"No, I have a few errands to run and I'll just go to the office after."

Sofia waved a hand at Annabelle. "I'll take care of him. Go change, AB."

She led Sebastian away, but not before Annabelle heard him question, "When did you start calling her 'AB'?"

It was a nickname that only Prudence, Greyson and Gabe had called her, then Devlin when they'd become close friends. Even her parents called her by her full name all the time. She hadn't known Sofia for that long, but wasn't upset that she felt comfortable enough to use her nickname. Annabelle lifted her arms and tried to wriggle the dress over her head. *Dammit.* She hadn't undone the corset.

Annabelle poked her head out of the dressing room door. "Sofia?"

Sebastian lifted his head. He was seated across from the dressing room, his suit jacket unbuttoned and his tie slackened.

"She ran across the street." He motioned toward the door with his head.

Fuck. "Can you please go grab an attendant for me?"

Sebastian smirked. "Are you squeezed in so tight you can't get out?"

She rolled her eyes. "The corset needs to be undone first."

He stood and slid his phone into his pocket, moving forward just a few inches. "I can do it."

"Oh, no, I couldn't bother you to do it."

"It's no bother, I'm capable of untying some knots."

She turned her body to show him the back of the dress. "Do you know what a corset is?"

"Of course I know what a corset is."

"It's much less complicated than untying knots."

"In that case, let me do it for you."

He continued forward and motioned for her to come out of the room. She had no good reason to say no, not if she wanted to get the dress off and get on with her day anytime soon.

"Okay, thank you," she said, with more gratitude than she thought she could muster. She turned her back to him, feeling exposed despite being fully covered up.

A shiver ran through her when the tips of his fingers grazed the nape of her neck, a soft caress, brushing aside a tendril of her hair that had fallen from her bun. He moved closer as he worked on the knot, his head bent far enough down that his warm breath wafted over her shoulder. Without being able to see Sebastian, her perception of touch was overwhelmed. The slight shift of his body, something that she wouldn't notice any other time was now amplified. His heat radiated onto her as he stepped even closer, his fingers deft at loosening the corset. He went slower than she imagined he would. She'd hoped for perfunctory assistance, but rather she got a sensual lesson in sensory overload, every atom in her being focused on the spot his hand was touching at any given moment.

Row by row, he hooked one finger under the corset strings to loosen them. His other hand gripped her waist, holding on for purchase, flexing and loosening as needed. One particular tug knocked her off balance and her hand shot out to brace on the dressing room door and she bent just a little at the waist. Her body stilled as her ass came in contact with Sebastian's front, much closer than she realized. He didn't react, but his work became jerky, moving her back and forth with each yank, brushing against her each time he did. Her insides turned to liquid and pooled at the center of her, and she didn't notice a short time later that he had stopped his movements.

"You're undone." His voice was low and hoarse and still too close for comfort. Comfort stopped a long time ago.

"Thank you," she stuttered and bolted into the dressing room without a backward glance, shutting the door and leaning against it, her breath coming out fast. She knew he was still on the other side, and he only moved away when she heard Sofia's voice questioning what he was doing.

She changed back into her usual work attire and opened the door when she thought she was ready and had herself under control.

"Oh good, you got help with the corset," Sofia said.

"She got help." Sebastian coughed. "Are you coming out to lunch with us?"

"No, I really do have errands to run, and if I'm coming back to work this afternoon I need to get them started now."

"I guess I'll suffer his company alone," Sofia joked as Annabelle walked to the door.

"Winters." Sebastian's voice stopped her. She wasn't ready. She was emotionally spent after earlier and didn't want to deal with him right now. Nevertheless, she turned and their eyes locked. She saw a hunger in his depths that she wasn't prepared to analyze, but it was there, raw and aching. She waited. For what, she didn't know.

"I need you to drop my dry cleaning off, are you going downtown or uptown?"

She huffed out a laugh and the tension snapped like a rubber band. Her only response was to flip him the bird and walk out of the store.

Chapter Ten

Annabelle Winters in a wedding dress.

Sebastian swallowed hard. He remembered each move she'd made while twirling in the mirror. But most of all, he remembered her face, before he'd gone and ruined her moment by speaking.

She'd been a vision in white. Or off-white, he couldn't remember now. All he saw was the longing in her eyes. The joy when her hands had floated over the bodice, touching the swell of her breasts with gentle fingers before skimming down to her waist. Then the joy turned to sadness. After a moment her movements went from caressing to jerky and sharp. He wanted to know why.

He also wanted to know why the hell he'd offered to unlace her corset. Of all the stupid things he could've done, he'd had the great idea to get too close to her. Too close to her naked back. When she'd lost her balance and braced herself with her hand, it was all he could do not to lift her skirts and take her right there. Bend her over and bury himself inside her, all the way. More than all the way, if there was such a thing, and he wanted to make it a thing.

Sebastian was playing a dangerous game with desire. If he'd thought imagining what her nipples felt like gave him a raging hard-on, her actual ass against *his* raging hard-on yesterday was almost enough to make him come on the spot. The simple act of touching her skin, so softly, because he didn't want her to know he was touching her for pleasure's sake, had been enough to excite him, and when she pressed herself against him, it had been the most exquisite torture.

Finishing off the workday had been painful and a cold shower when he got home hadn't banished her from his mind and he'd ended up taking a long swim in the lake. Exhaustion had won in the end and he'd slept well, awake early and ready for the town softball game.

The softball game was Amber Falls' kickoff to the weeklong Summer Solstice Celebration. Sofia wanted to play — he thought Annabelle had talked her into it — so here he was, throwing a softball back and forth with someone he didn't know, trying to act happy that he was outside at ten a.m. on a Saturday morning. Sweat was running down his back because the humidity level was already higher than it was in Satan's mouth.

Annabelle wasn't at the ballfield when they arrived. It was clear Sofia had taken a liking to Annabelle, against all his warnings, and was becoming friends with more people in town than he even knew. He wasn't at all surprised when she insisted on walking to Annabelle's to get her.

Sebastian threw the ball into his glove a few times before tossing it back to his throwing partner — Sam, he thought he said his name was. He'd been greeted by name by quite a few people and a small fissure of shame opened up that he didn't know who any of them were. One woman had asked how the corn crops across from his house were doing and he hadn't known how to answer.

Anonymity was a crutch to him. The less people know about you, and the less you know about people, the better. But this was Amber Falls, a small town like no other, where everyone's business was your business and vice versa. So, he'd answered that the crops appeared as healthy as corn should be and tried to think of something to ask her but drew a blank. She was oblivious to his silence and continued to talk, telling him about her dear husband's eczema problem until Sam asked him if he wanted to warm up.

He didn't want to be there, but the day was nice and he hadn't done much outside his own property since he'd gotten to Amber Falls. Restlessness was setting in, so his decision was made. While he'd never admit it to anyone, least of all himself, he wanted to be around Annabelle, and this was the place to do that. Then, she walked into the park and when Sam threw a ball to him it sailed over his head, both the ball and the warmup partner forgotten.

Annabelle's uniform clung to every curve she had. The pants hugged her ass, and he could almost mold her shape in his hands. The top Annabelle wore was tight, the buttons pulling open over her chest, offering him a peek at the skin inside and a glimpse of a very pink bra. She was a small woman and the heels she wore everyday brought her up to a height that closer to his. Today, she was wearing tennis shoes, which knocked about five inches off where she usually stood. He liked it.

"Tell me how this works," Sofia was asking Annabelle as they walked over, both ignoring him.

"The whole town knows when we play and whoever shows up can join a team."

"What are the teams, though?"

"It depends on who comes. Sometimes it's businesses against businesses or adults versus kids, whatever the demographic ends up being."

Sofia shouted, "Guys against girls!"

A chorus of female cheers went up, and the teams were chosen. Sofia jogged off to join a group of ladies gathering in one dugout and Annabelle turned her attention to him, the ponytail that was pulled through the back of a blue Amber Falls baseball hat swinging with the movement.

"You're going down, sir."

Sebastian could help it. At these euphemistic words, his gaze traveled down her body then back up. He took his time—he wanted to make her sweat, to throw her off her game before they even started. He wanted to make as hot and uncomfortable in her own skin as he was in his.

"Game on," he answered. Oh, the game started a long time ago.

Once things got going, Sebastian thought less about Annabelle and more about winning. If he lost, Annabelle would hold it over his head and he couldn't have that.

"Go, Mr. Locke," someone shouted from his dugout as he stepped into the batter's box. He'd struck out the first time and singled the second, only for the next batter to end the inning with a pop-up.

Annabelle was playing second base, and so far they hadn't had to interact during the game. He was center field and only a few balls had gotten that far out there. Determined to drill the ball this time, he dug his toes into the dirt and choked up on the bat. The ball was thrown, and he swung with all his might, hitting a line drive over first base.

He might have been held to first, but the right fielder bobbled the ball, and he kept going, thinking he would round second and extend the single into a triple to bring the men close to scoring for the first time in the game.

He stepped on second base with his right foot, and he was sprinting to third when he found himself flying through the air and falling headfirst into the dirt, his right knee taking the brunt of the fall. Spitting to clear the dust from his face, he tried to figure out what had happened. He was running and had a clear path after he rounded second. While playing it back in his head for the third time he saw a foot stick out, the same one that tripped him, causing the fall.

Rolling over onto his back with a wince, he saw an angel leaning over him. Not a blonde-haired angel with a halo and wings, but a dark haired, vengeful one with a smirk on her face.

"Shoot, sir, you fell," the angel drawled, not acting the least bit upset at the fact.

"I didn't fall, Winters, you tripped me." He tried to move his leg and pain shot through him. Nothing that wouldn't be okay after he walked it off, but she didn't know that. He let out a huff as he tried to sit, satisfied when she turned serious.

"Are you hurt?" She reached out a hand to help him up and he moaned as he tried to put pressure on his leg. "Can I go get an ice pack?"

"I think I broke something or tore something really bad."

"I didn't mean to hurt you." There was a tremor in her voice. *Good.*

"I was running at full speed, what did you think would happen?"

"You'd stumble, maybe, but not break a leg."

He pulled his hand from her grasp and walked around her in circles, her eyes widening at the ease of which he was moving.

"Are you serious, sir? You were faking?"

He stopped, close enough to her that their uniforms brushed, and lowered his mouth to her ear. "I don't fake anything, Winters."

He saw her swallow hard and backed off.

"Watch it, now. I've got my eyes on you."

"As long as that's all it is," she answered and moved off to her base and the game continued.

The next inning, Sebastian was moved to first base and Annabelle had just hit the ball. He just wanted to pull her off the bag, to pay her back for tripping him and when he reached out his hand he meant to grab her uniform. A fistful of material was all he needed to put her off balance, but he missed. Big time. His thumb tangled in a bra strap as they moved, plastering the rest of his hand over a plump breast, her nipple pebbling in his palm.

They did a slow-motion dance, but he was doing a waltz while she was doing the cha-cha and their feet twisted, missing the beat. The toe of Sebastian's cleats stubbed against the base, and they tumbled to the ground, Annabelle moving the wrong way at the last second, falling face down on the ground with Sebastian on top of her. Her anger was vibrating off her onto every inch of where they were plastered together. His hand was still covering her breast and he gave an experimental squeeze, much against his will, not even aware he was doing it until Annabelle bucked beneath him, her lush ass pushing right into his groin, setting every sense in him on high alert. *Now this is familiar territory.*

"I can't breathe, you oaf! Get off me!"

There was no way she could mistake his erection and an uncharacteristic wave of embarrassment flashed through him. He pulled his hand away as though he'd been singed, untangling without incident from her bra strap now, and sat having to brace his arms on his knees to hide the bulge in his too tight softball pants.

"I'm sorry, Winters, I just meant to pull you off the base."

"Did you also mean to grab my boob?" She massaged the offended body part.

"Of course not," he spat back. "That's not enough to tempt me." He was lying through his teeth and the hurt that flashed through her eyes was enough to dampen his libido.

"My breasts aren't here to tempt you, sir." She pushed away his hand that he'd offered to help her up.

"What happened?" Sofia cried, running toward them and pulling Annabelle up. "Are you ok, AB?"

"I'm fine," Sebastian groused, "thanks for asking."

"Of course you're fine," Sofia replied. "Your head is hard enough to crack plaster."

"I'm okay, I'm okay," Annabelle insisted, turning her fury to Sebastian and getting in his face. "This idiot tried to pull me off the base."

Sebastian stood his ground, not the least bit intimidated by a woman who came up, maybe, to his armpits. "You tripped me earlier. It was a fair play."

"You didn't have the ball in your glove, the pitcher overshot it into our dugout."

Sebastian was surprised to see that she was right and no ball was in his glove. "It must've flown out when we fell."

"It did not," Annabelle seethed. "I was safe, and you pulled me off that bag out of spite."

"Spite? Why would I do that?"

"Because you can't stand that the men are losing."

He threw his hands in the air. "You think I care who wins the Amber Falls community softball game? I could care less about this shit and you know it."

"Hey, guys," Sofia tried to break in.

"You care about this shit enough that you'd risk injuring me to win," Annabelle accused.

"Only because you started it. Every single thing this town does is ridiculous and I'm only here because my sister begged me to come with. I have no interest in any of this."

"Guys, everyone is watching you," Sofia's voice was more urgent this time.

Sebastian took a breath and realized he was inches from Annabelle and the rest of the players were watching their display with disappointment on their faces. He stood to his full height and this time did take a full step back.

He could try to say he didn't mean it. That small-town antics weren't above him and he cared enough about the people here to make a sincere apology. He could tell Annabelle that he didn't mind her getting chummy with his sister, or he didn't experience a jolt of lust every time she was near enough to touch. He would mean none of it, so he stayed silent. He watched the clouds roll across her eyes, anger at him for being who he was.

He could have apologized, instead, he doubled down.

"I don't want to see you except for at work. This experiment with being friends has failed."

"We have a cake tasting tonight, or has your experiment with being friends with Greyson failed too?"

Sebastian's stomach clenched at these words. She wasn't being fair.

She continued. "You've made it very clear that you don't care about this town and now you're saying you don't care about your friends too? Are they just placeholders until you can move back to Georgia? You promised Greyson and Prudence that you'd do this."

"I'd like to make it clear that I *am* doing this for them."

"That's obvious, you idiot. Are you going to do it for me?"

"The only thing I'd do for you is write a semi-professional reference after you're fired."

"Oh, please. The Bee would fold without me and you know it." She ran a hand over her uniform and touched a foot to the base, looking expectantly at the grocery store manager who was playing the umpire. He had no choice but to call her safe as the ball had come nowhere near first base in all the commotion.

"Your move, sir. Or do you have other unsuspecting women throw to the ground?"

Sebastian shook his head. He'd let her bait him all afternoon and was over it. "Your name fits you. You're cold, Winters."

Chapter Eleven

The game was over, and the women had won. Sebastian limped off the field, trying to hold it together long enough to not show Annabelle he was in pain. It was enough that he'd had to play like he wasn't hurt for the rest of the game, he just wanted to get out of her presence, so when Sofia said she was going to Annabelle's afterward he didn't try to stop her.

Sebastian didn't want to go home yet and found himself walking down the street when his phone rang.

"Locke."

"Sir, I'm glad you answered," his assistant's voice came over the line. He started every call with the same words. "Washington is back on the table, the sale fell through, and Mr. Locke wants to know your thoughts on it."

"Why couldn't my dad just call me?"

"He's busy and asked me to."

He loved his dad, but some of his business habits annoyed him.

"Stevens, I'm in the middle of trying to run Locke Communication's first newspaper, and Mr. Locke wants to know if we're ready for more?"

Silence filled the line. "So, that's a no?"

"No, that's not a no. Tell him I'll think about it and get back to him."

He ended the call then felt a moment of chagrin for hanging up so abruptly.

Sebastian's life focused around work. Being in Amber Falls didn't stop his workload from Atlanta from following him home after hours. Thank goodness his dad only slept four hours a night. The man had boundless reserves of energy and never lost an ounce of dedication to his work. Sebastian kept up with him the best he could, but sometimes it got to be too much.

He was tired now, thinking about having to go cake tasting with Annabelle then having to dig back into the Washington newspaper's finances after. He had a bit of time before he needed to meet her, so he walked to Finnegan's, hoping to find Gabe or Greyson, cursing when he remembered both his friends were out of town. He was there anyway and could use a drink, so he sat in an empty seat at the crowded bar, nodding to the bartender who walked over to him. He must've been new, the same one who'd mistaken Annabelle and him as a married couple.

"What can I get for you?" the bartender asked.

"I'll take a whiskey, neat." He thought for a beat as the bartender reached for a bottle, his knee throbbing. "You'd better make that a double."

The bartender poured the spirits into two tumblers, obviously mistaking Sebastian's request, and he didn't correct him. He could drink it just as well out of two glasses as he could one.

He nursed his drink and thought about what Annabelle had accused him of, that his friends were an experiment, and he would pick up and leave for Atlanta when it suited him without a backward thought. He knew that wasn't true. If seeking out Gabe and Greyson this afternoon spoke of anything, it was that they'd become almost like family to him. Friends came and went throughout his life, from classmates to co-workers, they filtered through as he moved on from school to work.

Gabe and Greyson, and to an extent, Prudence and Devlin, were different. He liked their company, wanting to know what they were up to and how they were doing, being as active a participant in their lives as they were in his. Annabelle, he knew through them. She kept her personal life very private, but it had started to creep in on him, hearing snippets of what she was like from her friends.

He tried so hard to separate Annabelle from Winters.

Annabelle was an enigma. She loved her friends and family with a ferocity that made him ache, but there was something deep inside that made her tick that he wasn't privy to. He wasn't allowed to see the real Annabelle. Sure, he saw glimpses of her, a flash of joy in her eyes or a cheeky smile, but they were fleeting and far between.

Winters was a hellcat. She was good at her job, a professional without reproach, but she caused bedlam whenever they clashed. If she had it her way, they'd do nothing but clash, caught in a perpetual cycle of arguments and conflict. *I like a good fight, and she's a worthy opponent, but I'm exhausted.* Always on his toes, or looking over his shoulder, wondering when she was going to pounce. Not able to let down his guard when she was around as she was sure to catch him in a weak moment and eviscerate him.

The problem was, as he spent more time with her, forced into her proximity outside of work, the lines between Annabelle and Winters were getting blurred. Sofia befriending her didn't help as he trusted his sister's judgment when it came to people, Stavros nonwithstanding. Now he'd seen her in a wedding dress and that had put him in a dangerous spot, coming close to mixing with Annabelle with Winters in his mind, and that was territory he wanted—no, needed—to avoid.

The air next to him stirred, and he glanced over to see Wyatt Reed pulling out the bar stool next to him and sitting. Wyatt sighed and Sebastian pushed his second tumbler over to him without a word.

Wyatt took a long sip and exhaled. "Women."

The meeting was a lot like when he'd first met Greyson and Gabe. He'd been at the bar, having a halfhearted conversation with Gabe who was bartending when Greyson walked in. Sebastian had known him from the movies—he loved the Ben Stone series—but he knew a little bit of what being in the public eye was like so he'd played it cool. He'd kept up his part of the conversation with Gabe, only finding out when Greyson kept joining in that they were brothers, and a friendship had been born. Maybe he wouldn't have become their friends if he'd known they were so close to Annabelle. If he'd only gone home that night, he wouldn't be forced into her company outside of working hours—which were hard enough as it was to deal with.

"Yep," Sebastian answered.

"A summer of celibacy doesn't seem so bad now, does it?" Wyatt asked.

Sebastian wasn't sure how to answer him. In his mind, abstinence was never the answer. Why cut yourself off from something so good? True, he hadn't had sex since he moved to Amber Falls—the college town demographics was a challenge. A lightbulb clicked in his head. Was he so hard up for Winters because he hadn't had a meaningful release with anyone other than himself? That must be it. The lack of sex was making him crazy, crazy enough to have carnal thoughts about *Winters*.

He sat in companiable silence with Wyatt while he surveyed the bar, surprised at how many people he did know, by face if not by name. There had to be someone for him here.

He saw the cashier from the bank, but she looked happy to be holding the hand of her husband. The ticket girl from the theater was wrapped up with her partner, both women coming up for air at the same time. He cringed as he saw the elderly receptionist from the mayor's office. He might have to rethink his take on celibacy.

"Prospects haven't been too good around here. Besides, this is temporary until I move back to Atlanta." Against all rationality his chest squeezed at the thought of leaving Amber Falls.

Wyatt gave a solemn nod. "So, either you're not putting down roots or you can't have the one you want?"

"Can it be both?" Sebastian joked.

"Someone once told me that you don't need entanglements to have fun." Wyatt shot him a pointed glance.

"That someone was an idiot."

The door behind the bar that led to the kitchens swung open just then.

"Who's the idiot, now?" Leo, Finnegan's cook, asked as he set down a plate of onion rings in front of Sebastian. "Hey, Wyatt, good to see you, man."

"I didn't order anything." Sebastian pushed the plate away. His stomach was still roiling from his latest encounter with Annabelle, and he didn't think he could eat greasy bar food, no matter how good of a chef Leo was.

"I know you didn't," Leo responded, "but I saw you out here all glum like someone kicked your puppy and I know how much you like my onion rings. I thought I'd try to cheer you up."

"Any other day I'd take these and be thankful, but I don't think I can eat anything right now."

Leo raised his eyebrows in question to Wyatt.

"Women," Wyatt explained.

Leo slid the plate over to Wyatt. "I get it, man. My wife woke up this morning and decided that we needed to redo our entire backyard and started doing everything and expected me to go along with her like I knew all along what she was planning. Like raising three kids isn't enough, I have to add landscape architect to my resume."

Sebastian felt like shit. He'd talked to Leo many times over the months he'd been here, but not once, apparently, had he cared to *talk* to him. This man had a life, a full and busy life, from the sound of it, and he knew nothing about it.

"I'm sorry, Leo, I didn't know you had a wife and kids."

"Don't worry about it." Leo shrugged. "I don't have main character energy."

"What the hell is main character energy?" Sebastian asked.

Leo gestured to Wyatt, who had just raised an onion ring to his mouth.

"Main Character Energy. The people that can't help but enthrall everyone around them. The ones that people flock to whether they want them to or not."

Wyatt chewed and nodded. "That's a good explanation. I wish that it wasn't all or nothing in the entertainment industry. Not everyone craves the spotlight."

"Some people do, some people don't, but you can't help the vibe you give off. It's like the saying goes—some people were born to be a star—they draw everyone around them in. Then there are the Leo's of the world. We're the background characters that are just there to fill up space."

Leo's explanation didn't sit well with Sebastian. Who had made Leo feel like he was just a background character? Yeah, there were actual movie stars in Amber Falls and that would overshadow anyone, but he had a wife and three kids. He was *the* main character in their lives. Who needed the world to flock to you when you had that?

The unanticipated thought made a wave of nausea rise in him.

A wife? He'd thought years ago that he was husband material but that had been dispelled when he'd asked Serena to marry him and she'd all but laughed in his face. And kids? That was as foreign of a concept to him as quantum physics. He might have once pictured himself a married CEO, and a trophy wife was all he needed to shine at the endless dinners and cocktail receptions his job required him to attend. Kids had never been part of the equation.

"What are their names?" Wyatt asked.

"Leo Jr, is five, Brittney is three and Samuel was just born last month."

Sebastian's stomach sunk even lower than it had been. A wave of something akin to embarrassment washed over him.

Maybe Annabelle was right. Maybe everyone here was just a placeholder, filling up pre-designed spots in his life until he left for good and went back to Atlanta. He finally recognized the emotion. Shame. Shame that he was taking the people in his life for granted, even those who he only knew peripherally. This wasn't an emotion he was familiar with. He made decisions daily and was confident in all of them, so this foreign reaction rising within him left him deeply unsettled.

"That sounds wonderful," Sebastian admitted with a truthfulness he didn't know he possessed.

"I'm not complaining." Leo took the empty plate from Wyatt. "I love every second of it, even if I never sleep anymore," he called as he walked back into the kitchen.

Sebastian and Wyatt sipped their drinks in silence, watching a baseball game on TV, until he noticed the time.

"Shit, I'm late."

"For what?"

"I'm meeting Winters for cake tasting."

"Is Winters the woman?"

Sebastian pushed his stool back and stood, downing the rest of his whiskey.

"The one and only," he confirmed. He paused, then clapped Wyatt on the back. "It was nice to hang out with you today. Let's do it again."

"I'll be around," Wyatt replied, his air of mystery still intact.

Chapter Twelve

Annabelle stood in the bakery, Love and Flour, waiting for Sebastian, who was supposed to meet her here fifteen minutes ago. She'd changed out of her softball uniform and was back to wearing her reliable armor—a pin-striped dress shirt, pencil skirt and heels, rounded out by her trademark bun.

"You're late," she snapped as he walked in the door.

"And you're observant," Sebastian shot back.

"Don't test me, sir. Let's get this over with."

"Gladly." Apparently neither of them were in the mood to be in each other's company.

"Ah, the happy couple!" A woman sailed out of a back room, her caftan flowing behind her.

"No!" Sebastian and Annabelle shouted in unison.

"We're helping the happy couple," Annabelle explained. "They had to leave town."

"Oh, yes, I see now. You're not Prudence and Greyson."

"We are not," Sebastian confirmed. "We're here to pick out their wedding cake, though."

"Follow me." She gestured for them to go through a door. "I have the cakes they pre-selected all ready. I'll leave you to it, let me know if you need anything." She shut the door and they were alone.

"Should we start with the lighter flavors first, so our palettes stay clear for the heavier ones?" Annabelle pulled one of the chairs out and sat, grateful that she was back to business, operating as if she was helping him choose the layout for a Bee issue. The longer they stayed professional, the longer they could be in each other's company.

"Are you allowed to eat this much sugar? You're not cheating on a diet?"

Annabelle buried her head in her hands and took a deep breath. She wasn't going to let him goad her into any bad behavior. She'd be professional and they'd be done here soon.

"Goest and fucketh thyself, Your Highness," she muttered.

Whoops.

He stilled as he sat in his chair. "Did you just speak to me in Regency?"

She raised her head and pierced him with her gaze. "How would you know what Regency is?"

"I'm a publisher. I read everything, including Regency Romances. Don't get off the subject."

"If anything, I was speaking Shakespearean."

"Do you feel the need to speak Shakespearean often?" He looked around the room, apparently feigning concern. "Do you see Shakespeare here with us now?"

"Just—" She stopped and blew her breath out. "Let's get this cake tasting done so we can get out of here."

"Whatever you say."

Annabelle moved the cakes into the order she wanted to taste them and waited for him to do, well, anything.

"Do you have a preference on flavors?"

"I'm more of a salty guy."

"Yes, I'm well aware of that."

Sebastian rolled his eyes. "Let's start with the vanilla."

The rest of the cake tasting turned out to be an exercise in self-control for Annabelle. She was sure that Sebastian wasn't trying to make each bite he took erotic, licking his lips and making sounds of pleasure when he tasted one he particularly liked, but it sure as hell was accomplishing it. He had the knack for making her go cold then white-hot, but this was something that had only just started happening to her. She had to think of something that would take her mind off wondering what his tongue, the one that just licked rogue icing off his top lip, could do to her.

"The layout for next week's edition needs some improvement."

Sebastian paused with a forkful of some chocolate concoction halfway to his mouth.

"You want to talk about work?"

"What else would we talk about? Do you want to go over what happened at the softball game?"

Her tone was mocking, but her palms were sweaty. She'd done the opposite of taking her mind off Sebastian and now she could only think about how his hand had molded over her breast and the way her body had reacted when he'd given it a squeeze. She remembered in detail how he felt on top of her, his unmistakable erection pushing into her backside, long and hard, pulsing. The sensation of wanting to lift and open for him so he could take her from behind hadn't gone away.

Her breath quickened and she could feel her face start to heat up.

"No, I want to talk about work," she insisted, desperate to stop thinking about Sebastian and sex.

Sebastian shrugged. "Sure."

Annabelle narrowed her eyes. "I don't like this new, appeasing part of your personality."

"It's not new, it's just a part of me you've never seen before."

Her mind flashed to other parts of him she hadn't seen before. "I don't like it."

Sebastian set down his fork and sat back in his chair.

"What's so wrong with me letting you get your way?"

"Letting me?"

He quirked a smile. "Yes, letting you."

Annabelle's ire rose. She knew he was baiting her, but she couldn't help but to defend herself.

"No one *lets* me do anything. I make my own decisions and I'm in charge of me, no one else."

"You're sounding a little too defensive."

She was being defensive, but she wasn't sure what to say. He was trying to get a reaction out of her, the blasted man. Instead of answering, she speared a piece of cake and shoved it in her mouth, allowing her time to think while she chewed.

She'd made the right decision to keep things professional between them. The more she stuck to work subjects, the less they'd delve into anything personal.

Sofia's arrival had instigated the blurring of lines between boss and employer, forcing them into contact with each other on a more intimate level. Until this week, she'd barely ever seen him outside of the office. After being stuck in the Atwood cabin this winter during a storm, she'd distanced herself when they got back, keeping a wide berth from Sebastian and only interacting with him when needed.

This latest bout of togetherness had started when she, against all better judgment, agreed to help him get his house ready for his sister's visit and had bled into Prudence and Greyson asking for their assistance. She knew she should've said no to Sebastian and made him deal with it himself, but she hadn't, and here they were. It was possible that their proximity in a small town like Amber Falls would've been inevitable, thrown together against their will despite her trying to keep her distance. It was *also* possible that neither of them cared to keep away from each other anymore. That was a reality she didn't want to explore.

She'd taken a bite of one of the last samples when she noticed Sebastian's eyes glancing from her eyes down to her mouth and back again.

"What?" she asked, darting out her tongue and finding some excess frosting on her lip.

Sebastian reached his hand out and extended his index finger to her and she froze. He touched the corner of her mouth, his short nail scraping her bottom lip as he swiped his finger over it. The tip of his finger was rough. Rougher than she would've imagined from someone who had a desk job.

It happened before she could stop herself. She was so tired of him trying to get her off balance or put her in a position where he thought he had the upper hand. Time for payback.

As he was bringing his hand down, she reached out and grabbed it with more force than she'd intended. His eyes widened in surprise. *Good.* He tried to jerk his hand back, but she kept an iron grip on it and brought her mouth to it, holding his gaze as she lowered her mouth onto his finger and oh so slowly sucked back up. A flush appeared on his cheeks and it only deepened when she swirled her tongue around the frosting at the tip of his finger before letting it out with a popping noise, satisfied with his apparent discomfort.

So much for not exploring that reality. She had a moment of doubt about her actions until Sebastian's now trademark smirk appeared on his face.

"You've wanted to do that for a while now, haven't you?"

The insufferable man! She couldn't even suck his finger like she'd suck his dick to throw him off his game.

"Get over yourself," she spat back, annoyed that she was annoyed.

"You've never taken rejection well, Winters, and I see you still don't."

"You rejected my book," Annabelle pointed out, "you didn't reject me."

"Exactly. It was business," he started to explain, but she held up one hand to stop him. If this is where he was heading, she'd follow along with him.

"You rejected my book in a way that no author should have to hear."

"I'm sorry but—" He stopped when she interrupted him once again.

"I don't want an apology."

"I have no intention of apologizing. I said it was business, and I mean it. I didn't even know you beyond the knowledge that you were an intern."

"Brian Smith set up the meeting. He told me you liked the book and were excited to meet me."

"Brian Smith is a self-serving, narcissistic waste of space. Let me guess — you turned him down for a date before he so magnanimously set up a meeting with the CEO of a publishing company?"

Annabelle felt sick. "He said he was your friend."

"We're friends like a vampire is friends with a virgin."

"That's an interesting comparison."

Sebastian shrugged. "It works."

Annabelle's head was pounding, and she didn't want to deal with him anymore today. She couldn't deal with Sebastian with his tight shirt, perfect hair and ass-hugging jeans. She wanted to get this cake tasting done, head home and burrow under her blanket until the sun rose the next day.

"Why are you so upset?" Sebastian's tone was low. "You're supposed to be a good journalist, roll with the punches, you know?"

"I am a good journalist," Annabelle hissed. "You, who has no patience for small-town affairs, came here and decided to change everything. You're in my friend group, you're changing the paper, and..." Annabelle trailed off, not sure where she was going with any of this.

"Things change, Winters." Sebastian paused for a moment then started again. "Everything changes. Sometimes for the good and sometimes for the worse, we just have to accept it." His eyes took on a faraway look as he continued. "I didn't want things to change, I wish things could have stayed exactly how they were. But that's life. I can't go back and change what happened in Atlanta, and we can't continue like this—" Sebastian stopped, his eyes refocusing on Annabelle, not realizing how close he'd moved toward her. He shook his head and leaned back. "It is what it is, Winters."

Annabelle couldn't help but wonder what he'd have changed. Clearly he regretted something, and she became uncomfortable, wishing she hadn't heard any of those words, hadn't heard the tone of his voice. The regret, even a hint of desperation. She preferred Sebastian as the emotionless boss, he wasn't supposed to have any sort of depth.

"None of that matters, sir." Annabelle wasn't sure who she was trying to convince with these words. "We're here to pick out cake, not re-hash the past."

"We've never hashed it out before, so how can we be re-hashing it?"

She raised her eyes upward. What on Earth had she done to deserve this man? Had she been a terrible person in a past life? Was she paying for the sins of her ancestors? Or was she just the unlucky object of Sebastian's current fascination?

She enunciated each of her next words. "What kind of cake do you think Prudence and Greyson will like? That's the only thing I'm concerned with now."

Sebastian held her gaze for a moment longer. "I always thought wedding cakes should be vanilla."

A jolt of surprise shot through her. "You've thought a lot about wedding-cake flavors?"

"I've been to a lot of weddings."

Annabelle cocked her head and took another bite of a lemon-vanilla-flavored cake.

"Fancy ones, I'd bet?" She pointed at the cake she'd just sampled with her fork. "I like this one."

Sebastian scooped up the rest of the piece. "Not always fancy. I guess I just know a lot of people."

Annabelle sensed a hint of annoyance behind his words.

"You know a lot of people, or a lot of people know you?"

Sebastian chuckled. "You're good. I guess having a publishing CEO on a guest list checks a lot of boxes."

Annabelle leaned closer, needing to dispel his self-deprecation. "No, I'm sure you're invited for your keen wit and sparkling personality."

"You know what? I'm going to believe that's true. Just for today I'll believe that people like me for who I am."

"Don't go too far, sir. You're still…you."

Sebastian laughed. "You know how to keep me grounded."

"I *am* friends with Greyson Atwood, if you recall. He's a pretty big name in Hollywood and I knew him long before he became famous. I've seen the people who use him just for his fame and because they think they can get something out of him." She shot him a thoughtful look. "I'm sure that's why you became friends. He saw a kindred spirit in you, someone else who might have been used for what they could offer other people."

"Now you're psychoanalyzing me, Winters?"

"I wouldn't dare, being in your company outside of work is terrifying enough, let alone trying to get into your head."

She poked a piece of cake as they sat in silence, swirling the frosting into a peak.

"Sofia is leaving in a few days. When she's gone, we can work on the gift registry."

"So soon? She just got here." Annabelle and Sofia had formed a quick bond during her visit and she was sincere when she'd told her she was sad to see her go.

"Yeah, she wouldn't tell me why, just that her time to go was here."

"Well, shoot. I was hoping to get some more fashion pointers from her."

Sebastian eyed her up and down. "What kind of pointers do you need? You wear the same clothes every day."

"You should know. Just because one wears a suit every day doesn't make it the same suit."

"You have a point."

"Of course I have a point."

He gestured to the cake on the table. "So, what do you think?"

"The lemon vanilla. It's perfect for a late summer wedding, crisp and clean."

"You're sure? Crisp and clean is how I like my laundry, not my cake."

"You know what I mean."

"Do I? Because I don't want Greyson and Prudence coming home to a wedding cake that tastes like —"

For the second time that afternoon, something came over Annabelle. She would describe it later as an out of body experience, where she saw herself pick up a piece of cake and shove it into his face. The shove wasn't gentle, either, and as she smeared it over his mouth and nose, he grabbed her wrist, with a lighter touch than she'd taken his.

"Why did you do that?" he growled.

"I don't know what came over me," she sputtered, shocked at her actions.

He dropped her hand and picked up a napkin. Why the *hell* had she done that? As if she needed to give him any other ammunition against her, now she was shoving cake into his face? She'd never live it down.

"Sir, I'm sorry, it's just that you made me—"

"*I* made you?" An incredulous tone spilled out of his mouth.

"No," Annabelle backtracked, "of course you didn't. I have no excuses."

Annabelle was mortified. She'd lost her cool—again—with Sebastian and needed to leave, to get out of his presence.

"Just order whatever cake you want, I'm sure it'll be fine." She grabbed her purse and a napkin and stood, almost knocking over her chair in the process.

"Winters," Sebastian called, halting her in mid-step. She didn't turn, not wanting to hear whatever he had to say. "I never said I didn't like it."

Her only response was to slam the door behind her.

Chapter Thirteen

He'd liked it. A piece of cake had been shoved into his face in anger, and he'd liked it. They'd had an actual conversation, one that hadn't relied on one-upping each other with insults. Sure, it was a short conversation, but it had been one, and he'd gone and ruined it.

He didn't know what had come over him, why he'd needed to insult Annabelle by comparing her taste in cakes to his tighty-whities. He was better than that. Any woman he'd dated knew he was better than that. He was a gentleman, someone who deferred to the fairer sex on a regular basis, but this one woman knew how to push all his buttons and push them hard. Annabelle was so cold and impersonal most of the time, all business and no play. The only time he was able to break through her hard shell was when he goaded her into it. The hot passion that he knew simmered just below her surface would bubble up and he'd get scalded every time, but he liked it. *Psychoanalyze that, Freud.*

"You're thinking about her, aren't you?"

Sebastian and Sofia were on the way to pick up Annabelle. Sofia's rental car had engine troubles, and it ended up being perfect timing because Sebastian and Annabelle needed to work on Greyson and Prudence's gift registry, so they'd opted to drive Sofia to Amherst instead of getting her a new rental. It was also terrible timing, because he would be forced into Annabelle's company for the shopping trip and the drive home. Just them. Alone.

"No, why would you think that?"

"Because you're not listening to a word I say."

"I haven't done that since you were born, why would I start now?"

"Very funny." Sofia shot him a sideways glance. "But you are, aren't you?"

Sebastian heaved out a sigh. "I'm going to miss you, you know."

"Yes, I know you will, but I'll be back before you know it."

"You're ready to come back to Amber Falls and you haven't left yet?"

Sofia nodded. "This town pulls you in. It's peaceful. That's why you're staying, isn't it? You can be yourself here, you don't have to be Sebastian Locke, publishing CEO, heir to the Locke Communications empire?"

Sebastian thought about this and recalled his words at the softball game and realized that the people here let him be. They didn't want or expect anything from him, and he liked that.

"It's true, I'm able to do my job without any of the extras."

"You know, a place like Amber Falls would be great to find someone to hang out with."

He didn't miss the crafty look that crossed her face, but he decided to play along.

"I've got plenty of friends to hang out with. In fact, you've met them all. Multiple times."

She reached over and punched his shoulder. "You know what I mean. We had a good example of love growing up and despite everything that could pull a high-profile couple like Mom and Dad apart, they stuck through it all."

"We did, didn't we?" Sebastian agreed.

"Yes, so take their example and run with it."

Sofia had spent a good deal of time with only one other person in Amber Falls, and Sebastian no longer liked where this was going.

"I don't run with scissors, Sofia."

"Just point the blade down so if you fall, it isn't fatal."

He was saved from having to reply when he pulled up to see Annabelle waiting in front of her building.

As Annabelle walked to the car, Sebastian's next words to Sofia rushed out.

"Keep your opinions to yourself, please."

"I'll make no promi—hey, AB! Thanks for coming along."

Sebastian scowled, annoyed to hear Annabelle's nickname come out of his sister's mouth again. "You didn't answer me the other day when I asked when you started calling her 'AB'?"

"It's what my friends call me, Sir," Annabelle replied for Sofia, buckling her seatbelt.

"Yes, I know that, *Winters*. I'm wondering why my sister is calling you that." He couldn't help but lean into the use of her last name.

"Believe it or not, I'm capable of making friends in adulthood."

"It seems a little desperate to call your boss' sister your friend."

"Sebastian!" Sofia seemed genuinely shocked at his words.

He looked into his rearview mirror, surprised to see a grin tugging on Annabelle's lips.

The rest of the drive was uneventful, and he could only imagine that it was so because he kept his mouth shut while they talked. He listened. Not something he was used to—he was used to giving the orders and running the show, but he took this time to listen to Annabelle and soak in how she reacted with his sister—with someone she actually liked.

They soon reached the Amherst airport, pulling up front to drop Sofia off. Sebastian pulled her into a hug after he got her luggage out from the trunk.

"I'll miss you, little sister. Come back soon."

"You're in love with Annabelle Winters."

He dropped his arms from around her and hoped Annabelle hadn't heard her. "I take it back. Go far away from here and never come back."

Sofia just laughed and hugged Annabelle goodbye—he hoped without giving her any similar parting wisdom—and waved as she walked to the sliding doors.

"Text me when you get there," Annabelle called, opening the back door.

"I'm not going to play chauffeur the rest of the day, get up here," he snapped, trying to shake Sofia's words out of his head.

She slid into the front seat and Sebastian shifted gears and pulled back into traffic. The store wasn't very far, but Annabelle's bare knees caught his eye. As she shifted in her seat, her skirt hiked higher up her legs, legs that were longer than anyone her height had any business having. She crossed her heeled feet at the ankles, angling herself toward Sebastian. The skin on her legs was smooth as silk, creamy with a slight tan.

He saw a scar on her right knee, and he longed to reach over and lay a possessive hand over it, to stroke the scar with his finger, soothing it from any past trauma. His mind took over and in the secret place, a place he didn't want to admit existed, she didn't protest, and he would take hold of her legs as he drove. She would shift herself in the seat, opening for him, asking him without words to inch his hand further up until it teased the hem of her panties, and he'd stroke one finger over her covered opening, and she'd already be wet with need. He'd ease the panties aside and gently touch her —

"Sir?" Annabelle's voice broke him out of his thoughts, and he heard honking behind him. "The light is green."

He pulled into the intersection, cursing himself for allowing his mind to go to a place he needed to avoid like his life depended on it.

Grasping for a subject that would take his mind off his new proclivity to put his hand up her skirt, he noticed that she was twirling the ring on her right hand.

"That's an interesting ring."

Annabelle looked at it then held her hand up, still twirling it with her thumb.

"It's been in my family for a long time. Nothing fancy, but I like the simplicity of it."

"It doesn't look impressive at first glance, but there's some intricate detailing if you give it a closer look."

"You've spent some time looking at my ring?"

Sebastian shrugged. "I noticed it. I always notice good workmanship."

"Then you should stop giving Sofia a hard time."

"Where is Sofia going?" he asked. "She was vague with me."

"Oh, here and there," she offered just as vaguely. "She's a very talented designer, you know."

"I've seen some of her dresses."

"Then you know she's got to go where her passion lies."

Sebastian shifted in his seat, uncomfortable once again, his mind going back to wandering hands and panties.

He eased into a parking spot at the store then waited for her to come around to his side of the car before making their way inside.

"You're too quiet," Annabelle said after they got the necessary equipment to zap the items to put on the wedding registry.

"I'm trying not to think too hard about my sister's passions," he deflected from the real reason for his silence.

She nudged him with her elbow. "C'mon, be serious. You have to see how talented she is."

"Talented? Yes. Driven? No."

"Ouch." She pointed down an aisle. "Here, let's go this way."

"Yes, but the truth. Sofia has always taken the easy way to get what she wanted. The fashion thing hasn't been handed to her on a silver plate, so she's stalled."

"Kind of like getting handed a publishing empire to run?"

"Double ouch." Sebastian pretended to be wounded as he selected a flatware set.

"That was uncalled for, I'm sorry."

"It's like you live to take digs at me." He sounded more petulant than he'd intended.

Annabelle's hand lingered for a moment too long as she took the registry gun away from him as they wandered down an aisle filled with Southwest-themed knickknacks.

"That's not true."

He shot her a look.

"That's not entirely true," she amended. "I also live to take you down a peg *and* to put you in your place."

He couldn't help but laugh. "I believe all of that."

Their newfound camaraderie was short-lived, and they lapsed into an awkward silence, Annabelle's heels clicking on the floor the only sound as they picked more items for the registry.

"Did you know Leo is married and has kids?" he asked, wanting to keep their conversation going.

"Of course. We talked about it when I turned in my PTO form for Samuel's baby shower in April."

Sebastian felt himself pale when Annabelle mentioned the PTO request. Although she hadn't brought them up again since he'd admitted they were fake, he knew she still hadn't forgiven him.

"I'm sure we did. It was a long time ago."

Annabelle's eye narrowed. "Maybe you should fill out a PTO request, if it's time you're looking for."

He swallowed hard. This conversation was not going the way he wanted it to. "I'm sorry, I don't recall it," he said in hopes they'd move on. He should've known better.

Annabelle stopped in the middle of the aisle. He'd fallen a few steps behind and almost ran into her. "We had a whole conversation about the possibility of starting a baby of the month column, and Samuel would be our first baby if we went with it. We had an entire business lunch when we talked about it."

Sebastian remembered that business lunch. Annabelle had spilled red sauce on her blazer and when she'd leaned forward to take it off to dab water on it, she'd put the swell of her breasts on full display for a split second. Whatever business they'd discussed he couldn't recall.

"I have a lot on my mind, Winters. Besides, talking about kids isn't in my conversational wheelhouse.

"You don't want kids?"

I should've just taken the silence as a win.

"That's not what I said. None of what we're talking about is my personal preference or take on anything marriage or child related. I'm just here to help my friends."

"Well, you're the one that asked about Leo."

"But seriously." Sebastian let himself tip toe back into the field of conversational landmines. "He's got three kids. I didn't know any of his personal life."

"Sir, we've had this conversation many times. You just don't care to know anything about anyone. You do what you need to do for business and go home to your lair at the end of the day to, I don't know, do whatever villains do in their lairs."

"When I get home I have a whole night of work ahead of me. My job doesn't end when the newspaper part of the day is over."

He swore he saw pity flash in her eyes. Pity was never what he wanted to see flash in a woman's eyes.

"Really? You go home from work every night and work some more?"

"Most nights, yes," he admitted.

"You weren't lying at the Atwood cabin, then. You never do get to unplug."

When they'd gone to the cabin in January there had been no cell phone reception. The first night, without emails or text messages to keep him up, he'd crashed harder than he'd ever remembered and he'd slept like a baby the rest of the nights.

"Silver platters can be exhausting."

Annabelle reached out and clasped one of his hands in hers.

"I didn't know," she explained. "I was flippant and obviously don't know the amount of work you have to do."

A lightness washed over Sebastian at her words. He'd held in a lot over the years, from the despondency he'd gone through when Serena broke his heart, to him working nonstop so he didn't have to think about it anymore. To have someone know and acknowledge this lifted a burden he didn't know he was carrying. *I like you.* The words formed in his mind and almost escaped his mouth before he bit his cheek to stop them. He *liked* Winters?

Their hands were still entwined, and realized this might be the first time they'd touched willingly. Yes, it had all been leading to this one moment in time, every choice they'd made put them in this exact spot. He ran his thumb in light circles over her skin and watched as she took a deep breath. It wasn't the time to tell her, though. They couldn't get through a few minutes without arguing and he'd have to work on that before he could confess his like.

"Now." She untangled their hands. "Let's finish this off and get out of here."

His vulnerability had seemed to open the barrier between them, and their conversation flowed as they completed the rest of the registry.

On their way out of the store, he held the door open for her, his hand coming to rest at the small of her back, a gesture he loved to do, as if that was the most natural place for it. They passed a poster with large letters boasting *Do your wedding registry online!*

"You realize we could've done this online? That Grey and Pru could've done this all online?"

"I had an okay time," Annabelle admitted. "I don't think I wanted to kill you more than that one time."

"I'll take whatever progress I can get." He was flippant, but he meant it. If progress meant he'd need to turn on the Locke charm, then he'd crank that as high as he could go.

They stood behind his car, the light from the midday sun highlighting every strand of color in her hair.

"Well...I guess I'll see you later." He walked to his door, glad that they'd gotten to spend this day together.

"Sir."

His heartbeat raced as he turned back to her.

She was standing with her palms up, the usual mask of annoyance back on her face. "We have to drive back to Amber Falls. Together. Did you forget we're a hundred miles from home?"

Shit. Well, it was nice while it lasted.

Chapter Fourteen

Turning on the charm was harder than he expected. After his feelings jumbled together and his sense scattered yesterday, he was still trying to put it all back together. He found himself drawn to Annabelle at work. She'd walk by his office, and he'd be out of his seat ready to follow her before he turned himself around and forced himself to sit and focus on his work. During an afternoon meeting in the conference room — a meeting with the advertisers that would keep the paper in business — he'd zoned out when he heard Annabelle's laugh come from down the hall. He wanted to know who was making her laugh and why she never laughed with him when he realized the room was quiet and waiting for him to respond to a question.

Finally, during lunch, he was able to see Annabelle without making up an excuse to be in her presence. He rounded the corner into the break room, after not finding her in her office, and stopped so fast he was surprised his shoes didn't make a screeching sound.

Annabelle was bent at the waist at the open fridge, rustling around for something on the lowest shelf, her bottom wiggling in a tight skirt.

"Damn," she muttered, straightening up and peeking in a Tupperware container. She gave it a tentative sniff as she went to the sink, almost dropping it when she saw Sebastian standing there, silent, like some sort of weirdo watching women sniff Tupperware. She dumped the contents into the garbage and started to wash the container, glancing over her shoulder.

"Can I help you, sir?"

Oh yes, she could help him all right, but right now he just needed to be with her, in the same room.

"Can you stop into my office when you have a chance later?"

"I can. I'm on a deadline and it might not be until after five."

"That's fine, I'll be here for a while still."

"Okay, I'll come when I'm done."

Sebastian didn't leave. He didn't want to leave.

"Did your lunch spoil? You can share mine if you'd like." He held up a brown paper lunch bag, thankful for whatever foresight told him to grab it before heading to the break room, and gestured to the table, pulling out a chair.

Annabelle wiped her hands on a towel, hesitation clear on her face.

"C'mon," he goaded her. "I brought ham salad."

"Well in that case, I can't say no."

They sat together while he split the sandwich and bag of carrots between them.

"Mmm, this is delicious." Annabelle swallowed her bite. "Where did you get this?"

"I made it," Sebastian admitted, and a glow flowed over him at her praise. "It's not complicated, though."

"I don't picture you as a guy who makes his own food. Other than the delicious eggs we had at your house."

"I enjoy cooking when I have the time, but this was pretty simple."

"Simple is okay when it tastes this good." She picked up a carrot and chomped off an end. "Don't you eat in your office most days?"

"It felt claustrophobic today. I'm lucky I found you in here." *Oof, rein it in, Locke.*

She didn't answer him but focused on finishing her meal. He tried to think of a topic of conversation, one that would bring them back to their easy communication of yesterday, but she was done and standing before he could come up with one.

"Thanks for the food. I'll stop in when I'm done with my story?"

He hoped he didn't look crestfallen when he nodded to her. It had only been one day since he'd realized he might like her, and he was already acting like a man starved for her company.

He tried to keep his mind off her the rest of the day, and he was surprised that he was able to get his work done when he saw it was already seven o'clock. The office lights were off, and he was alone. She'd forgotten him. He couldn't keep her off his mind, and she'd left without stopping in.

He sat back in his chair and stretched, disappointment flowing through him when he heard heels clicking in the hall. His body tensed in response and didn't ease when Annabelle stepped into his office.

"Sorry, sir, I lost track of time. I'm glad I caught you. What did you need?"

That's a loaded question if I ever heard one.

He motioned for her to come sit across from him, taking the time to think up a reason he'd wanted her to come see him.

"I've noticed morale is low around here and I wanted your take on it," he finally offered.

Annabelle appeared thoughtful. "We need to have some sort of team-building exercise," she decided.

He didn't know what response he'd expected, but that wasn't it. "Can I just hand out Bee logo travel mugs?"

"Trust me when I say no employee wants a travel mug with their company logo on it."

Sebastian tried not to go back to their old habit of arguing. "What's your idea?"

"Maybe a game night?" She pointed to a game of Monopoly on one of his shelves. "Where did you get that?"

"Gabe said I could take it. I guess I forgot I had it." He hadn't forgotten. He'd asked Gabe if he could take the game, hoping he could get a rematch in with Annabelle after she'd trounced him at the cabin this winter.

"You wanted a daily reminder that I beat you in Monopoly?"

There was no arguing, then there was not letting her walk all over him. "I *let* you beat me at Monopoly."

"Now that's bullshit and you know it."

"Whatever you say, Winters. You keep believing you could beat me. However you need to get through your day."

"Prove it. Let's play again."

Sebastian held her gaze. "Okay. But let's raise the stakes."

"Why would you raise the stakes on Monopoly? The thrill of winning is all I need."

"But what do you get from winning?"

"The satisfaction that I bested you yet again at something."

The next words were out of his mouth before he could stop them. "How about you have to remove an item of clothing instead of paying rent?"

A clearly stunned Annabelle stood with her mouth agape.

"Why would I agree to that? There's nothing in it for me."

Yes, Sebastian, why do you want to do this? He couldn't explain it, not even to himself, even as the new sensory memory of Annabelle's breast in his hand from the other day popped into his head. He'd thought about it so much — the hardness of her nipple, her ass pushing into his erection — he was reliving it all over again and needed more from her. His realization that he liked her emboldened him.

"I dare you."

Her eyes narrowed and he knew he had her — she'd never back down from a dare — so he was surprised when she stood and left his office. He loosened his tie, swallowing hard at the thought of a half-naked Annabelle. Maybe it was for the best if she left, he had his memories to relive after all, that might need to be enough. He didn't mind playing with fire, but this was jumping headfirst into a volcano. He'd just resigned himself to a night of no Annabelle when she reappeared. His pulse jumped when she walked back into the office a moment later and his cock jumped when he heard the click of the lock on his door.

"No one else is in the office, I checked," she explained her brief absence, walking over to the sitting area in his office as she talked and took the game down from a shelf. "I'm going to win, but I'll protect your sensitive ego and not let anyone know how much clothing you lost in this bet."

She motioned for him to join her at the coffee table in front of the couch and bent over, opening the box, her tight pencil skirt hugging her ass just like it had earlier in the kitchen. He prayed his arousal wasn't showing and composed himself for a moment by taking out a bottle of whiskey and two glasses from his desk drawer before standing.

"Are you trying to get me drunk, sir?"

"I know better than that. You could drink me under the table."

"That's accurate. Do you want to use money, or will clothes be our only currency?" she asked as she set up the board. She'd sat on the floor, her legs folded under her, so he took the couch across from her. Her shoes were next to her, already removed, and he didn't want to point out the error in this move. He had many more layers of clothing and by taking off both shoes, she had a scant amount that could be removed before she became indecent.

"I like money," he answered.

"Then we can pay for rent like usual, but remove an item of clothing as well."

"On hotels, not just any rent."

"High stakes, I like it. You can go first, sir. What token will you be?"

"I'll take the battleship." He reached for the piece and placed it on GO. "And you?"

"I'll stick with the top hat, it always seems to bring me luck."

"You'll need it, Winters." Sebastian settled himself on the couch and rolled the dice.

They played for an hour and the sun was setting by the time Annabelle got her first hotel. A smile bloomed on her face that had until then been the picture of concentration. It wasn't long until Sebastian landed on this space.

"What's your choice?" Annabelle was practically bouncing with apparent glee.

He waited until she calmed down. "I'll start with a shoe."

She startled at this and looked at her own feet. "I didn't think of that when I took them off."

"I noticed, but I wasn't going to tell you."

"Well played, sir."

Sebastian removed his shoe and they played on. Annabelle built hotels much sooner than him, and another hour later he was down to his shirt and pants while all she'd had to take off was her watch and the pin holding her hair up. Her long hair had tumbled down her back like a waterfall and he realized that he hadn't seen her with her hair down before. Every time he'd been with her, even at the Atwood cabin, she'd been put together. Seeing her hair down, and realizing he might see her even more disheveled, made his pulse race again.

Annabelle landed on one of his hotels and assessed her outfit. Whatever she removed next would bear a lot to him.

"What's it going to be, Winters?" His whole being stilled in anticipation.

She stood and twisted her body, clearly trying to figure out what to do next. She held his gaze for a brief moment before slipping her hands under her tight skirt and rolling down her stockings. She put one foot on the table and slowly slid one down her leg before putting her other foot up and just as slowly sliding the other down. He sure as hell wasn't going to tell her that she only needed to do one at a time and he watched her with rapt attention. She finally held up the sheer stockings and dropped them on the table.

"Done."

Sebastian wanted to blame it on bad luck that he landed on her hotels two rolls in a row, but the board was more hotels than houses at this point.

"What's it going to be?" she echoed his previous words.

Shirt or pants. Those were his only two options before he would be down to his underwear. He wanted to keep his pants on for as long as possible, otherwise this game would be over very soon, so the shirt it was. He didn't mean to go slow, but he was mesmerized by her stare as he released the buttons. Her tongue darted out when he pulled the shirt out of his pants and exposed the hair that led down to his cock and her eyes darted up to his before dipping back down. This was a dangerous game.

"Do you want to continue?"

"I won't lose," she insisted. "I have Boardwalk and Park Place."

Sebastian was strung as tight as a bow, and Annabelle was plucking him like an expert archer. One more pull and he was bound to either snap or hit the bullseye and he didn't know which one was worse. He sat back down and took a healthy swig of whiskey. "We'll see."

She rolled a double on her next turn, landing on a property without a hotel, but had the bad luck to land on a hotel next. Her hands hovered over the button on her skirt before she moved them up to her blouse and shrugged.

"A shirt for a shirt."

She removed hers faster than he had and he didn't have time to. A scrap of lace was all that covered the alabaster expanse of her chest. The bra was cut low, and he could see the dusky red of one nipple peeking over the top. This game wasn't dangerous, he amended, it was lethal.

He forced himself to concentrate back on the game and picked up the dice, praying that he could avoid her hotels, because once he took off his pants he wouldn't be able to disguise his erection. *Damn. Boardwalk.*

"Sorry, sir." She didn't sound sorry in the least.

Sebastian stood. He wasn't a shy man. He had a good body and nudity had never bothered him. Now? He was as nervous as a whore in church to remove his pants in front of Annabelle Winters, the one woman who vexed him more than any other. The only thing that spurred him on was the flush he could see spread over her. With her shirt off and the pitiful excuse for a bra covering her, he could see a pink blush move from her face down to her chest and under the lace. This excited him to no end. Her unflappable exterior wasn't hidden and he could see she was clearly affected by him.

If he had been slow to take off his shirt, he must have barely moved now, unbuttoning his pants and zipping down his fly with the speed of a sloth. Annabelle was still kneeling on the floor across the table from him, in the perfect submissive position where she could take his cock right into her mouth and swallow it to the hilt. He dropped his pants, his briefs tenting out, unable to control his erection.

She rose to her feet and bent toward him. When she reached forward, his breathing stopped, anticipating where her hands would end up. He didn't expect her to take his mortgaged properties and the rest of his cash and hold them up to his face.

"You lose."

She dropped them into the middle of the board and gathered up her items, walking shirtless and barefoot to the office door. After unlocking the door and opening it, she turned back to him.

"Sir." And closed it with a soft click after her.

Chapter Fifteen

Annabelle was insane. Well, she'd had an insane moment last night, when she'd won the game. Sebastian Locke — her *boss* — had stood in front of her in all his barely concealed glory, and she'd wanted to stay. The madness was brief, but it had been there, to stay and see where the rest of the night took them, already half-naked and tipsy on whiskey. In the cold light of day, she was glad she'd had the fortitude to leave him standing there. Really. She was.

She hadn't thought far enough ahead when he'd challenged her to the game last night, hadn't considered that she'd still have to work with him every day, and coming into the office in the morning felt like a walk of shame even though she'd bested him once again. It didn't feel like she'd won. She'd spent the night tossing and turning in her bed, running her hands over her overstimulated body, imagining what his cock looked like. She'd almost seen it last night. It was large, that was for sure, and her mouth had watered at the thought of taking it deep into her mouth and sucking it back up to the tip, like she'd done to his finger at the cake shop.

This was her last thought as she passed through the door of the Bee in the morning. Sucking her boss off. So, it came as no surprise to her that he was standing at the front desk talking to Mrs. Johnson. His eyes bore into hers as she sped past him, and she was sure he knew, in detail, what she was imagining in her head.

She reached the elevator and pushed the button, willing it to come down to the first floor as she heard him approach her. She stabbed the button multiple times as if that would make it move faster as he came up to stand beside her.

"How's it going today, Winters?" he asked.

"It's going well, sir," she answered, her voice too loud.

Sebastian glanced back to the front desk and smiled at Mrs. Johnson. "Are you okay? You seem...agitated."

"I'm nothing of the sort. I'm fine."

The elevator dinged as it opened in front of them and he gestured for her to proceed ahead of him. The smile stayed on his face until the door closed and he turned to her.

"You left a mess in my office last night." His voice was low, reverberating through her.

"You mean I left you a mess?"

"No, I don't. You knocked over the whiskey bottle in your rush to leave. It seemed like you couldn't wait to get out of there."

"I beat you for the second time. I didn't need to stay any longer than that." She was full of false bravado.

He held her eyes for a long moment, as if daring her to break. "You're sure about that?"

"I'm sure about every decision I make," she answered as the elevator opened on the fourth floor and she stormed to her office, slamming her bag on the desk. She couldn't stand Sebastian Locke so what the hell was she doing playing strip Monopoly with him and imagining giving him a blow job?

No. She'd be lying if she said she couldn't stand him. Something had changed — everything had changed — over the last few days. He'd stopped being her adversary and had turned human on her. A human that she might want to know better.

She wished Prudence or Devlin were here. Hell, she'd even talk to her mom, LuAnne, if that meant getting everything off her chest, but she tossed that idea out the window as fast as it had blown in. LuAnne would turn into the worst of the matchmaking mamas if she knew Annabelle held even the barest hint of feelings for someone.

Feelings? No, it was nothing more than a raging libido guiding her right now. What did that say about her, that she was letting herself be governed by something so basic, like she couldn't control her growing attraction to Sebastian?

She was saved from having to answer herself by a knock on her door.

"Come in."

The door cracked open and Renee, one of the features editors, popped her head in.

"Hey, Annabelle, I have a huge favor to ask you."

"What's up?"

"I know you assigned me the write-up on the movie night tonight, but Eva is sick and I just can't make it."

Annabelle was grateful to have a distraction tonight rather than sit home, alone, with her unwelcome thoughts.

"That's no problem, Renee. I'll get the article done."

"Thank you so much. Let me know when I can repay the favor."

Annabelle waved her off. "Don't worry about it. Just make sure Eva gets better and that's good enough for me."

Renee thanked her again and left, shutting the door and leaving Annabelle right where she didn't want to be. Alone with her thoughts.

The day — and her thoughts — had got progressively hotter. By the time work ended and she stepped outside, she knew she had just enough time to shower and change before the first movie started.

The humidity made itself known as soon as she left the office despite her short sundress, and the short walk from her condo to the park didn't help. The park was filled with families as the first showing was always of a kids' movie, and she found a spot near the back, between two pine trees, hoping a breeze would funnel through at some point. Laying her blanket down, she sat and pulled out her pencil and paper and started taking notes for the article.

She felt a tug of longing in her gut as she watched the families around her. Her quick conversation with Sebastian about kids the other day was still fresh in her mind. She'd put a focus on her career but there was an emptiness inside her, one that even a Peabody award couldn't fill. She fiddled with the hem of her short dress and took a long drink from her water bottle, trying to dispel her now pensive mood and jot down things that could help her write the article. She was doing just this when a shadow passed over her notebook. There hadn't been a cloud in the sunny sky today, and she looked up to see Sebastian standing over her, shading eyes that had crinkled at the sides with a smile.

"I never took you for an animation fan, Winters."

"No, I don't watch many kids' movies. I'm writing the article for Renee."

"She did say Eva wasn't feeling good in a meeting earlier today." He motioned down to her. "Is there room on your blanket for one more?"

Annabelle willed the blanket to shrink, but alas, it stayed just big enough for two.

She shrugged. "Go ahead." Her calmness masked her disquiet at his appearance.

He sat next to her, a little too close. As if the heat of the day wasn't enough to make her swoon, she now was enveloped in his heat as well.

"Did you bring any water?" she asked, lifting her now empty bottle.

"I didn't think about it."

"They're selling bottles over there," she offered, wanting him to leave, even if just for a few minutes so she could catch her equilibrium.

"Hydration is key. I'll grab you one too."

He loped over to the water stand, his long legs eating up the distance. She took him in, casual in khakis, a white T-shirt and sneakers. *He looks good* was the only thought she could process, and he was back before she could gather herself like she wanted. When he sat back down, he seated himself just as close to her. Maybe closer than before. She willed herself not to move away and got used to his nearness during the first movie. They made small talk throughout, but were for the most part silent while they watched, and she wondered if he was just as distracted by her as she was by him. She was happy to accept the flask of whiskey when he offered it to her, her lips touching where his had just been.

They were sitting at the very back of the group of moviegoers, and by the time the movies switched over to the feature film the families had all left. Dusk had pushed out the sun filled skies and the black and white film that had just started lent an intimate setting, turning the night into a sepia filter. Inch by inch they'd drifted closer to each other as the night progressed and as the actress on the screen lifted her skirt to show off her leg in an attempt to hitchhike, Sebastian's hand came to rest on her thigh, and he trailed a path with his fingers up to the short hem of her dress. His gentle touch caused her skin to prickle into awareness, a shiver running through her.

She was already hot—she'd been hot since he first sat down—and was now starting to get bothered. The temperature had barely cooled after the sun had set and the humidity in the air made her slip dress cling to her sticky body and her hair moved every so often with the promise of a breeze that was never realized. The night was too still and she felt electricity in the air.

Annabelle moved her hand and hooked her pinky over his. She tried to look at him without turning her head but couldn't see what she wanted to, so she tilted her face just so and saw him lick his lips, his dark profile blending in with the night sky.

She knew now that he wasn't unaffected by her. After the Monopoly game last night, and the impressive erection he'd almost bared to her after losing, she was certain that the attraction that had been growing in her was also growing in him. Something was growing. She was emboldened by this and flipped her hand over, threading her fingers through his. She heard a sharp intake of breath at her motion, and he turned to her, a smile curved on his full lips.

"You're not paying attention to the movie, Winters," Sebastian accused, but he circled his thumb in a hypnotic pattern on her hand and she was surprised that such a small motion could excite her.

"I stopped watching ages ago," she admitted.

"What's distracted you?"

"It's not obvious?"

He leaned closer to her, his breath mingling with hers, which had started to come out a bit faster.

They stayed that way for a few moments, millimeters from each other, until Sebastian closed the distance and his lips brushed over hers. He pulled back before moving close once more, his tongue teasing her into opening for him. She hesitated for only a second before letting him in. The tension that had built since the softball game and during Monopoly last night finally broke and she moaned.

Their tongues clashed, swirling, invading then retreating. It was a sensual battle of her senses and she needed to be closer than right next to Sebastian. Without breaking their kiss, she hooked her leg over his and straddled him, her skirt getting pushed up as she pressed herself into him. She rocked forward, every nerve in her body screaming for more. More friction, more speed, more everything. Sebastian's hands ran down her back and grabbed her ass, grinding himself into her. This was the more she needed. She tilted her head back and he ran his mouth down her neck, nipping at the sensitive skin, his teeth scraping and marking, but every second she was away from his mouth was too long. She wanted her tongue back on his, to taste the smoky whiskey they'd sampled earlier. She wanted —

A flash of lightning followed by a crack of thunder broke them apart. Annabelle jumped at the sound and scrambled to her feet moments before the sky opened and dumped rain down on what remained of the unsuspecting crowd. She turned her palms up, cupping them, trying to catch the rain or hold on to this moment she didn't know, but this moment slipped through her fingers just like the rain. Rivulets of water streamed off her down to a still sitting Sebastian. The rain had the effect of a cold bucket of water, and she snapped out of her lustful haze.

"This can't happen," she sputtered against the rain.

Sebastian stood and reached out to her but she backed away, tripping over the edge of the soaked blanket but caught her balance before she fell.

"Annabelle, wait," he started, but she didn't let him finish.

"This can't happen," she insisted again before turning toward the direction of her apartment and walking away.

Once she got to her place, she stood in her entry way, dripping onto the carpet, trying to process the kiss that had just happened. He was her boss. Not only her boss, but her arch nemesis ever since he moved to Amber Falls. *Arch nemesis? He's not a comic book villain.* She meandered her way to her bathroom, not caring that she was dripping water all over her hardwood floors.

"It wasn't supposed to rain," she muttered as she stripped off her soaked clothes, pausing after she'd pulled off her dress to stare at her face in the mirror, making a disgusted expression. "I also wasn't supposed to make out with my boss."

Annabelle grabbed a satin robe and had just thrown it on when she heard a knock at her door and the peephole showed her Sebastian was standing on the other side. A second knock sounded.

"Winters, I know you're here, I followed a trail of water leading to your door."

She hesitated, and after a moment she double knotted the robe for good measure and opened the door. He was soaked, his T-shirt clinging to his chest, showing the outline of a contoured chest and defined abs.

"How did you get into my building?" she asked.

"The office manager's cousin lives here, and he let me in."

Annabelle blew out a breath, letting her annoyance show.

"Why are you here, Mr. Locke?

"Why did you leave?"

"Don't answer my question with a question! Why are you here?" she demanded.

He stared at her for a moment before lowering his eyes. "I don't know."

"There has to be a reason you're outside my door," she pressed.

"I wanted to make sure you got home okay."

"I'm a big girl, sir."

Sebastian took a step forward, one of his hands starting to reach for her, but stopped. "I don't know what happened with that kiss, but I do know that I like you. It doesn't make any sense why I'm here other than I've found that I like spending time with you. I didn't want our night to end like that, with you running away, like you do every time."

"Every time? I—"

He did reach out at this, and laid a hand on her arm. "I don't want to argue. I won't let the night end like that."

She stood, watching him, the heat of his hand seeping through her robe. This wasn't the time to discuss his...feelings...for her. She'd just started thinking that she didn't hate the man, she couldn't process *like* right now.

"Then it will end like this. I'll see you tomorrow."

She shut the door, glad that she had the willpower not to rip off his soaking shirt and touch the muscles that had been outlined. She waited until she heard the ding of the elevator before pulling out her phone from her robe pocket and dialing Prudence. Depositing the phone on the kitchen counter, she grabbed a bottle of wine and started to fill a glass, not letting Prudence say anything after the call was answered, her words tumbling out in a waterfall of exposition.

"Pru, you will not believe it. I went to movie night tonight to cover for Renee who has a sick kid and guess who showed up? Sebastian, obviously. We've been spending so much time together with this huge list of things you left us to do, and he's okay to spend time with and you know he's kind of funny and it started to rain and we kissed and then I left and he followed me home and he said he likes me. Prudence, let me repeat that for you. He said he likes me!"

The only thing she heard on the other end was silence.

"Did you hear me? Sebastian Locke likes me!"

"Yeah, we thought that would happen eventually. It's about time he admitted it."

Annabelle set the wine bottle down a little too hard at the voice on the other line.

"Grey! Where's Prudence?"

"She's in the other room."

"Go get her!" she yelled.

"Not so fast, I have some good advice too, you know."

"Unless it's advice that hasn't come from one of your scripts, I don't want to hear it."

She heard him sigh.

"Ok, I'll go get her."

Annabelle downed her glass and was refilling it when Prudence spoke.

"Sebastian told you he liked you?"

She had to reiterate her words from before, but she slowed down this time.

"Yes. We've been spending so much time together finishing your wedding stuff and we've been getting along pretty well. Mostly. And then I had to go and kiss him tonight. Or he kissed me, I'm not sure who started it."

"Wow. I can't believe you guys kissed. Do you fancy him?"

"I find him tolerable."

"I'll take that. Tolerable is a few big steps up from despising, so it's progress."

"Wait. Why did Greyson say that you all thought we'd get together eventually?"

"You don't think you're the only one that can come up with a plan, do you?"

"Prudence Marie Hardwick, you set me up?"

"We set you both up. Devlin and Gabe helped to plan it, too."

"I don't believe I fell for it."

"You didn't fall for anything. I did need your help, but you didn't need Sebastian there for most of it. Grey put on a show when he asked Sebastian to help, too."

"I'll get you for this, Pru."

"Just give him a chance, AB. I saw the way he's been looking at you and I think his affections are true."

"What do you mean *the way he's been looking at me*? With disdain in his eyes?"

"With longing."

"Oh." Annabelle was taken aback by these words.

"Why are you so set against getting together with him?"

"Other than the perception that sleeping with my boss is wrong?"

"Yes, other than that."

"He's Sebastian Locke. We don't get along."

"Everything you've told me tonight contradicts that reason. Just give him a chance, will you? Whatever has happened between you two is in the past, and I don't want it to come between what could be a great future. Now I've got to go, Grey and I have this thing we need to get to."

"Fine, I'll do it for you."

Prudence's final words before she ended the call were, "No, do it for you."

Chapter Sixteen

Sebastian's self-control had gotten him far in life. It had stopped him from blowing a major deal when he was just starting out. It had pulled him back from the brink of making a fool of himself when Serena broke up with him. He didn't beg, he didn't plead — he took what he wanted without a second thought, with absolute controlled emotions.

Except for last night. When he'd reached out to Annabelle at her door and saw the flash of panic in her eyes, he'd retreated. He tapped into all his willpower, all his self-control, to not pull her back into his arms and continue what they'd started in the park. He'd followed her back to her house with less than honorable intentions on his mind, his need for her overtaking his common sense, but something in the vicinity of his heart had constricted at the pain on her face and his body had turned from being full of lust to being overrun with protectiveness.

His heart squeezed again, this time at the thought that she was so repulsed by him that she couldn't stand to even touch him, that she'd shrink back when he reached out to her. He shook his head to clear those thoughts. He couldn't comprehend that she'd be so turned off by him. Annoyed, maybe. No, the way she'd felt straddling him in the park last night was anything but repulsed. Her slow undulations over him, the way she grabbed his hair and the noises she'd made low in her throat were proof enough to him that she wanted physical closeness as much as he did, so her behavior at her condo had him ten shades of confused.

He needed to get out of the office, to get away from knowing she was in the same building as him and he couldn't do anything about it, so he walked toward Finnegan's, wanting to have a drink, but not wanting to have one alone in his office.

Sebastian had just walked through the door when he heard the familiar voice of Gabe in the back office. He was comfortable enough with his friends that he didn't think twice about going behind the bar and entering the room. He'd been here before, after all, when Sofia was in town during New Years.

"I thought it was you." He reached his hand out to shake Gabe's, then he noticed Devlin and pulled her into a hug.

"Sebastian! It's so good to be back." Devlin kept her arm around his waist. "We missed this place and you all so much."

A glow of happiness lightened Sebastian at being connected with Amber Falls. Almost like he was becoming a town regular.

"Come on out." Gabe gestured to the main room. "We were going to have a bite to eat before heading back home, join us."

"Sure." Sebastian led them to an empty booth. "I have nothing else to do."

"That sounds glum," Devlin said.

"I didn't mean it like that. I'm having a hard time concentrating on today, so I've pushed off everything and have been sitting at my desk staring at the walls." The glance between Devlin and Gabe didn't go unnoticed by him, but he kept his mouth shut.

"You shouldn't have too much free time. Grey and Pru left with you with quite the list. Ah, shoot, I'll be back." Gabe left the table at the gesture of the bartender.

Sebastian shrugged, addressing Devlin. "The list is all done."

"Really?"

"It wasn't that bad." Sebastian sighed and took a drink of the whiskey the bartender had just set down. "Honestly, I had a good time hanging out with Winters."

Devlin raised her eyebrows.

"It wasn't bad," he repeated. "We worked well together."

"Is…there any more to it?" Devlin's tone was searching.

He was overcome with the need to be unburdened, that if he put his feeling out into the universe all would be well.

"I like her."

Devlin reached out and touched his hand. "We all know, Seb."

"Am I that transparent?"

"You've done everything but pull her hair and dip her pigtails in ink."

"But she doesn't know?" Sebastian was confused.

"I've never met two people more blind." Devlin looked at Gabe behind the bar. "Well, maybe Gabe and I. Has anything happened?"

"We kissed during movie night," Sebastian admitted.

Devlin's eyebrows shot up again. "You kissed during family movie night?"

"After, when it was dark and during the second movie."

Silence fell over the table while they sipped their drinks, broken by Devlin.

"Everyone thought you two would get together."

"We're not together," he insisted, followed quickly by, "Everyone?"

Gabe slid back into the booth at Sebastian's last words. "I've known Annabelle for a very long time. She's never acted like this toward anyone, only you. I've never understood why she's this other person with you and toward you, but it could all make sense if there was a mutual attraction she's been trying to fight."

"You think so?" Sebastian's heart lifted, just a flutter.

"She's fighting something," Gabe said.

"Me." Sebastian downed the rest of his drink. "She's been fighting me."

* * * *

Later that evening he sat at his desk, the pink and purple light fading from the sky, and relived last night's kiss for the hundredth time. Sebastian tried to keep to himself for the rest of the day, pushing off all his meetings but the one he was supposed to have with Annabelle, which she ended up canceling via email. He wasn't going to question why, in fact, he was secretly glad she begged off. If he thought his mind had been in disarray after Sofia dropped her bombshell then left, today it was absolutely chaotic.

He ran a hand through his hair, his frustrated sigh letting out some of the energy pent up inside him. Annabelle had closed the door in his face last night then avoided him today. If she needed space, he'd give it to her. His resolve lasted for a moment before he stood from his desk and moved across his office. He felt a pull tugging him through his door and down the hall to find Annabelle.

A weight lifted off his shoulders when he saw her, sitting hunched over at her desk, pen in hand, marking what looked like a printed article. One hand gripped the pen while the other touched a piece of hair falling down the nape of her neck. He wanted nothing more in this moment than to free the mass from its clip and watch it cascade down her back. The literal undoing of Annabelle.

He watched her work, surprised she didn't sense him standing there. Her finger twirled the one strand of hair that dared to defy her bun and break loose. Twirling and twirling, hypnotizing him.

"What do you want?" she snapped.

Ah, so she did sense him. Satisfaction rushed through him at this, glad he wasn't the only one.

"Are you done with the article yet?" He knew this question would piss her off, but he was at a loss for what else to say. He'd never admit that he was drawn to her from his office like a marionette, and she was the puppeteer.

"Almost, I'm doing my final proof." Annabelle didn't look up, but she dropped the piece of hair, and he felt a pang of sadness for it, that it no longer knew her touch.

Silence stretched between them, sticky and uncomfortable. *Okay, then. Maybe it's time to poke the bear.*

"Deadline was an hour ago. I can't leave until you get that turned in so I can go over it."

She finally speared him with a withering glare. "The longer you stand there bothering me, the longer it'll take to finish it." She lowered her head back to her work. "Good day, sir."

"But—"

"I said, good day!" Her emphatic words shot across the room.

"You don't get to 'good day' me, not after what happened last night."

Her head whipped up so hard he winced with sympathy. "I rejected you, that's what happened last night."

"No, *I* walked away." He held his hands up in supplication. "You know what, I came here to apologize, not to fight. I'm sorry about last night. I'll be in my office when you're ready to turn the article in."

Sebastian turned on his heel and left. His strings were cut and he was left dangling. This wasn't going to work. They were oil and water, fire and ice, a cat and a mouse. Okay, yes, he'd poked the bear. He knew what he was doing, but it was the only way to get a reaction out of her. She was completely closed off to him otherwise, last night had proven that.

He walked into his office and shut the door, hoping to sever the connection to Annabelle. He leaned over his desk, his hands braced on the surface and his head hung low.

Fool.

He was a fool for thinking there could be anything between them, even after admitting to her that he *liked* her. Except for shoving her tongue down his throat last night, she'd never given any hint that she thought of him as anything other than a pain in her ass. She couldn't even bring herself to utter his name.

The door to his office slammed open and Annabelle stood there, her expression thunderous, like an avenging angel.

"You didn't walk away from me last night—*I* stopped anything else from happening." She stalked toward him with the stealth of an apex predator, and he was in her sights. "You don't get to apologize to me like you're some sort of magnanimous being, taking the high road. We *both* wanted it just as much, but nothing else will happen. The kiss was a one-time thing."

Annabelle had moved so close to him that the anger that radiated off her in waves washed over him. He towered over her, even with her in heels, and this height gave him a good position to glower from.

"Why are we arguing about this? Nothing else is going to happen," she reiterated.

Sebastian's control snapped and he took her hand, flattening it against the front of his pants. "This is going to happen."

"You can deal with that however you want."

"I want you to deal with it."

"You don't get to dictate me. I'm not your secretary, or one of your society misses."

"Do you think that's what I'm trying to do? Command you?"

"Isn't it? You run the show, it's what you do." She poked her finger into his chest. "You don't get to run me."

Sebastian's voice lowered. "I don't want to run you. I want you to run me. I need you to take things out of my power. Let me do something without having to be the boss."

Annabelle's chest rose and fell, a bellow of air forced out with each exhalation.

"Take me as I am," he pleaded.

Her eyes searched his, then closed in supplication, and she laid her head on his chest.

"I wouldn't want you any other way," she whispered, straight into his heart, and it didn't just soar at these words, it flew above him and summersaulted in glee.

He could tell that Annabelle was still wound as tight as her hair, and the satisfaction Sebastian got from unclipping it and letting it fall down her back rivaled that of what he knew was to come. The strands tumbled down, and he ran his fingers through it, a waterfall of silk. He needed more, so he turned her body and gathered her hair in a fist, running one finger along the delicate nape of her neck. Annabelle leaned her head back into his hands, her back arching with the movement, bringing her ass into contact with his front. He hissed through his teeth, the pleasure of her bottom cradling his cock was almost his undoing.

With one arm, he swiped the desk clear. Office supplies fell to the floor with a loud bang, and he realized that the door was closed, not locked, and neither of them had made sure they were alone. None of this mattered. The only thing reverberating through his head was that he needed her *now*. He needed to know the softness of her thighs, if she would be ticklish when he ran his hands up the inside of her legs to part her for him. The thought that anyone could enter the office was erased from his mind, replaced by the need to know how her legs would wrap around his waist while he pounded into her. Would she keep them loose, or would she pull him tight to her, urging him on? He had a singular focus now, and nothing was going to ruin this moment, audience be damned.

Blood pumped through his body, sluggish and molten. Every nerve was frayed and overstimulated and when she turned back to him and pulled up his shirt, the backs of her knuckles brushed ever so lightly against his stomach, he jumped, branded by her touch. It was too much. This was too much. He wanted to take it slow, but his body begged for release. Annabelle deserved to have him pleasure her at leisure, for them to spend hours learning each other's bodies, to atone for their past, but he didn't have the time. He had to possess her, and he had to do it now, without preamble and without finesse. His need for her outweighed any thoughts he could put into their coupling. This would be carnal. Pure and unadulterated fucking.

No, it was an absolution.

Sebastian brought her flush to him and backed her to the desk. He slid his hands up her thighs, seeking her skin. Annabelle writhed under his hands, and he rested them on her legs to keep her motionless — she clearly didn't like the inaction.

"I haven't stopped thinking about your cock since we played Monopoly." She unbuckled his belt, dragging one hand over the straining front of his pants. She traced the outline of his erection, and he was surprised his pants didn't split at the seams. When she pulled down his briefs, his erection sprang up. "If I didn't leave when I did, I don't know what would've happened. I spent the whole night wanting to know what it would taste like."

Sebastian had never heard anything so erotic in his life. "You're killing me, Annabelle," he groaned, his hips pushing forward into her hands.

Annabelle stroked him, light as a feather, making him grasp her hand to tighten her hold on his cock. She knelt then, her tongue darting out to lap up the pre-cum on the tip of his penis. She swirled it around the head before taking him so deep that he nudged the back of her throat and she hummed, the vibrations causing him to buck into her mouth before she slid back up.

"Well?" He had to know.

"Better than I imagined, sir."

He gripped her arm and dragged her back up to him, lifting her and settling her on the desk, her splayed legs now cradling him.

"For the love of all things holy, call me Sebastian."

She ran her hand up his chest — his shirt had become unbuttoned but he didn't recall when — thumbs grazing over the flat discs of his nipples. He hissed in a breath through his teeth and used all his famous self-control to stay still. She needed this, and he'd meant it when he said he wanted her to take control, to not expect him to run everything or be in charge.

Her hot breath seared his skin before she ran her tongue over the same nipple her finger had just branded, while her hand had taken up residence lower down, pumping up and down his cock.

She tilted her head. "Sebastian." The word came out in a rush, and she took a steadying breath. "Sebastian," she repeated, now with a confidence that made him push into her hands.

His name on her lips, after all this time, almost had him spilling into her, so he reached down and steadied her hands.

"After everything we've been through, we should take our time, wring every ounce of pleasure out of this." He searched her eyes, hoping to see more than just lust, wanting to hear from her that no matter what, this wouldn't be where they ended.

Annabelle ran her hands down his back, her nails scraping a path before settling on his ass. She pulled him closer, the tip of his cock nestling into her opening. She moved her hips, allowing him to touch her gossamer hair before moving back a scant inch.

"I don't want to," she admitted. "I need it hard, and I need it now. I expect you to make me scream with pleasure the next time, but now, I need you inside me."

Next time. The sweet, sweet words that he didn't know he was desperate to hear.

He slipped on a condom, took his cock in hand and positioned himself at her opening. "If you think I need more time to make you scream, think again." He thrust into her beckoning wetness so hard the desk moved backward. He steadied himself and ground into her, holding her so she wouldn't move away.

Mine.

The insanity of when he was around her, his compulsion to push her to her limits all came down to this. This one point where they were joined, where their bodies had become one.

Forever.

The base of his cock pushed against her clit and he shoved that thought aside, needing to focus all his attention on not orgasming as soon as he moved, on how to make her come before he lost all control. And he *was* going to lose control, there was no doubt about that.

The only sound now was their breathing, ragged and shallow. Somewhere in the distance he heard a door slam, but that heightened his senses. Annabelle's eyes widened at the noise, then she moved her hand down to where they were joined, circling her finger over her clit.

"Hurry," she urged.

Sebastian groaned and made a guttural, almost animalistic noise in his throat, then plunged his tongue into Annabelle's mouth to quiet himself.

She broke away and turned her head, her eyes screwed shut and her mouth open in a silent scream. Sebastian batted her hand aside and replaced it with his own. He wasn't going to let her come by her own ministrations, he was going to make sure she remembered this, that it was *him* who brought her to orgasm.

Annabelle's eyes glazed over and she leaned back on the desk, her hands supporting her, opening herself up to him, watching where he was touching her. Another door slammed and the sound of laughter drifted through the halls.

"Look at me, Annabelle," he demanded. "I want to see your face when I make you come." Control be damned, he needed to do this for her.

She groaned and lifted her head, spearing him with her gaze, and her muscles contracted around him with her climax. That was all his battered body could handle and he pumped into her over and over, hot seed spilling out of him. He didn't let up, though, a second wave was building before the first one was even over.

"Boss?" The words were shouted from across the building, piercing the office like an arrow.

Annabelle had lain back on the desk after her orgasm, opening her up to a new and deeper angle for him, and tried to pull away at this voice, but he held tight. He had to.

"Not done…" he croaked.

She paused a moment then wrapped her legs around him again in earnest, urging him to keep going.

A second and more powerful orgasm overtook him within seconds, and he collapsed over her, his breath coming out fast.

"That was…unprofessional," he stated.

Annabelle threw her head back and laughed, stretching her hands over her head. "You know what? I don't even care."

Sebastian lowered his head to her neck and breathed her in—sweat, sex and her—it was intoxicating.

She gave him a small shove. "But I don't want anyone walking in on us, either." She gestured down to her hiked up skirt and his pants, pooled on the floor. "At least we don't have a long way to go to get dressed again."

Sebastian ran his hands down her chest to her skirt pushed up to her waist. He slowly, so slowly pulled out his still half-hard cock, and shuddered as her body relinquished the tip. He rolled off the condom with a wince, the stimulation of touching himself after two orgasms almost overwhelming.

"The last thing I want to do right now is hurry, but let's get this all picked up and get the hell out of here."

Annabelle hopped down from the desk. "You've got it, sir."

He threw her a look over his shoulder as he bent to pick up the picture frames from the floor.

She blushed, something he would've guessed she was incapable of after what they'd just done, but he found it becoming.

"Sebastian," she amended, slipping back into her heels.

They'd gotten each other and the room back to rights when one of the staff writers knocked and poked his head in, just as Sebastian had tucked his shirt back in and was leaning over the desk next to Annabelle, both pretending to study a paper placed on top.

"Boss, I thought I heard something back here?" Mark, a new staff writer, said.

"Just burning the midnight oil," Sebastian explained.

"It's not quite seven yet, so there's a ways to go until midnight," Mark pointed out. "I don't have to stay that long, do I?"

"No, Mark, you go ahead and go home. I was just going to head out myself."

Mark turned to Annabelle. "Are you coming?"

Annabelle's face flamed red, and she was saved from having to reply by Sebastian speaking again. "We're just finishing up, you go ahead. I'll see you tomorrow."

Mark waved as he left, and Annabelle let out a snort of laughter. Sebastian ran a hand up under her skirt, finding the crease of her ass and moving a finger forward to dip into her center.

"Are you coming?" he asked, in all seriousness.

"I plan to."

"Where should we go?"

"Mine's closer."

"Mine's quieter," he countered.

"We don't have to keep arguing over everything."

"You're right," he acquiesced. "Closer is more important."

Chapter Seventeen

Annabelle had never heard a grown man giggle before, but that's what they were both doing after they crashed through her front door. She was light, so light, a million worries lifted off her shoulders.

Everything she had done in her life had led to this — a perfect moment of bliss. If someone had told her a year ago that she'd consider anything having to do with Sebastian Locke as perfect, you could lock her up and throw away the key, as she'd be certifiable.

"Do it again," she asked, wanting to remember this new, happy Sebastian.

They'd made it to her bedroom and were lying on her bed, Sebastian over her, propped up on his elbows. He broke away from nuzzling her neck to ask against her skin, "Do what again?"

"Giggle."

He stilled and raised his head. "I do not giggle."

"Yes, you do."

"That wasn't giggling, that was a very manly laugh." He had moved now to unbutton her blouse. "It was a deep baritone, the opposite of a giggle."

Annabelle helped him, shrugging her shoulders to get her sleeves off.

"It sounded a lot like a giggle to me."

"*You* may have giggled, I clearly chuckled, or maybe chortled."

She unclasped her bra and eased it off, her nipples pebbling when the cool air hit them. She tossed it to the ground and lay back onto the bed. "I think you'll find those mean the same thing."

"Oh, sweet Jesus, call it what you want. I have better things to focus on."

And focus he did—a singular focus on her breasts that left her panting and pushing down his pants, wanting more. He let her take them off but went right back to his apparently important work. His mouth replaced his hands now, sucking each nipple in turn, never neglecting the other one.

"Are you ticklish?" he wondered and ran his hand up her side, fingertips grazing one breast then moving higher.

Annabelle didn't want to laugh, she wanted to be stoic but couldn't help it when a sound escaped her.

"Now that's a giggle," Sebastian explained, a pleased smile crossing his lips.

She ran her hand along the side of his face, cupping his cheek, wanting to keep the memory of this smile, this specific smile, forever. It was a slow, crooked bloom, slightly lopsided and entirely sexy, like he had the most delicious secret, and she was the only one he'd tell it to. She would hoard the images and pile them one on top of the other each time he graced her with them.

They'd been at odds for what seemed like an eternity, and she still couldn't seem to wrap her mind around the fact that she was in bed with Sebastian Locke, and he was on top of her, making her body feel sensations she'd only read about in books.

"I'm overdressed." Annabelle was still in her skirt, the same one he'd pushed up in his office, and she was ready to get it off. "I want your whole body against mine, naked."

"I can help with that," Sebastian promised.

He ran his hand down her stomach, pausing when she giggled again, giving her the same smile, the one she was going to keep for herself, locked away in a place only she could get to.

Any sounds of mirth stopped when he dipped his tongue into her navel and pulled her skirt down. His mouth moved dangerously close to her soft thatch of hair and his hot breath skittered across her skin. She blinked once and her skirt was off, Sebastian moving lower, bypassing the place she needed him the most. He ran his fingertips down her thighs to her stockings.

"I dreamed of this after you took these off in my office." He rolled one side down, taking his time, his palms searing her skin until the first one came off. Her breath hitched when he started on the second, going slower if that was possible, and she writhed in anticipation, the ache in her building to a fever pitch.

She undulated her hips, asking him without words to touch her where she needed it, to ease the ache building between her thighs. He resisted, because of course he did — he wouldn't be Sebastian Locke if he did what she wanted — and instead moved to her other leg. His fingers slipped under the top of her stocking, nails scoring her skin. He rolled it down to her calf and stopped, trailing back up her thigh and she shivered, goosebumps raising on her skin.

"Touch me," she commanded, trying to keep a waver out of her voice, almost succeeding.

"No."

She moved in protest.

"Not yet," he amended, taking his tongue and this time licking his way up her thigh, so close to where she needed him the most, and when he stopped at the apex of her thighs she felt a rush of wetness and groaned at the sensation. That got him moving, her vocalization of her need, and he parted her lips with his fingers, his mouth hovering just above her clit. He blew a soft stream of air and she groaned again.

"Sebastian, please." She tried to move, to squeeze her legs together against the onslaught of sensations a mere breath caused her.

"Say it again," he demanded, circling her wet entrance with the tip of one finger. "Say my name."

"Sebastian," she gasped, and he plunged his finger into her, lowering his head to capture her clit as he pumped in and out and a fresh wave of lust flowed through her.

Annabelle watched Sebastian's head rise and fall and felt disconnected from her body. She was able to sense the pleasure he was giving her and to, at the same time, observe the two of them, strangers turned into enemies, now turned into lovers. It was almost too much to take.

"Oh, God, Sebastian." He'd crooked one of his fingers, hitting the right spot inside of her and she almost exploded into pieces of light, a galaxy expanding into the universe. She wanted him, more than she'd wanted anyone before, and she wanted him inside her when she came. She grabbed his hair and yanked his head up. "I need you inside me."

He kept up his ministrations for a few moments longer then pulled himself up over her. "Whatever you want, Annabelle. Say it and it's yours."

She didn't want to say that this was turning into more than a quick fuck for her, or that if she examined her feelings, she'd find that she would be content with smoothing out the lines between his brows, or holding him at night so he'd sleep and the bags under his eyes would go away. That she wanted to take the weight of the world off his shoulders and help him bear the burden of being Sebastian Locke. No, she couldn't say any of that. Instead, she rolled a condom onto him and urged him into her, letting her body tell him instead, to try to translate her thoughts into actions.

The relief she felt when he slid into her was fierce. Her body tensed at the invasion then relaxed into the rhythm he set, content to let her climax build after their furious coupling in his office. Planting her heels on the bed, she widened her legs, giving Sebastian free rein to move. He lifted himself up onto his hands, hovering over her, and watched his own cock slide in and out of her.

"Oh, fuck." He looked from where they were joined up to her, apparent bewilderment in his eyes. She could sense the confusion in him—she had it too—the connection that had held them together from the beginning was so strong now that it was almost a physical ache.

"Come for me," she whispered, and ran her hands over his skin, smoothing her hand down his back. Annabelle clenched her inner muscles, her orgasm starting to build, and he inhaled a sharp breath, his movements becoming erratic, and she let herself go.

He buried his head in her neck and jerked into her, over and over, and the joy in giving him this release overwhelmed her, her heart swelling with triumph. He wasn't moving, he wasn't lifting his head, so she ran her hand through his hair while his breathing steadied, bearing his weight in what she thought was more ways than one.

In time he moved to the side, removing the condom then brought her flush against him and pulled a sheet up to cover their cooling bodies against the chill of the air conditioning. She laid her head in the crook of his arm. He smelled of sandalwood. That was unexpected.

Annabelle couldn't bring herself to say anything yet—she didn't want to be the one to break the silence. They'd now made love twice in one night when before they couldn't be in the same room without arguing. The fine line between lust and hate had blurred so much that she was dizzy, and if she hadn't been lying down she might've tipped over from the inertia of it all. So, she lay there, her mind swinging back and forth, metaphorical whiplash at the last forty-eight hours. Two days ago they'd played strip Monopoly, yesterday they'd kissed, and now they'd consummated their loathing for each other.

Sebastian cleared his throat.

"This was not on my Summer Solstice bingo card."

She lifted her head. "Now I'm curious what *would* be on it."

"Oh, a kid throwing a tantrum at movie night, Leo throwing a tantrum about the food vendors, Greyson throwing a tantrum about how Wyatt is running his theater program."

"You throwing a tantrum about everything to do with the Summer Solstice Celebration?"

"That's the Free Space."

Annabelle laid her head back down and closed her eyes. The last few sleepless nights, kept awake by thoughts of the man who was now in her bed, were catching up to her. Lulled by the rise and fall of his chest, she cleared her mind and let herself simply be.

It could have been an hour a few minutes later when she heard a rumble.

"Did you keep writing?"

"Hm?" She thought she'd imagined his voice, dreamed that he cared enough to ask.

"After you left Atlanta. Did you keep writing?"

She took a deep breath, letting herself both wake up as well as formulate an answer.

"I've never stopped."

"Do you have an agent? What publishing houses have you submitted to?"

Annabelle was now fully awake and fully annoyed—old habits die hard. She sat and tucked the duvet under her arms, on edge with these questions.

"I haven't submitted anywhere else, if you must know."

He held up his hands. "Can we talk about Atlanta without anger? I don't see any sharp objects and there's no cake here to shove in my face."

Annabelle inhaled, held her breath, then exhaled her anger away. They were just questions, not criticism of her life. "I re-grouped after you threw me out of your office, I just haven't submitted anything else yet."

Sebastian sat up as well. "I cannot believe that you'd let me, of all people derail you from your dreams. Annabelle, look at me. You are one of the most fierce and independent women I know. These four or five inch articles that you give the Bee show that you're more talented than a lot of writers I work with."

Annabelle didn't know what to say at these impassioned words. She'd been operating under the assumption that Sebastian truly knew nothing about her, but it was clear that she'd missed his attention to her work. She couldn't let him know that his words hit her like she was a bullseye.

"My decision had nothing to do with you, Sebastian. God, you're so arrogant."

"Okay, I didn't mean for it to come out like that. What I meant is that you're talented, and you should pursue publishing if you want to."

"Please believe me when I said it had nothing to do with Atlanta. My major was in journalism, and I pivoted back to that when I saw there was a position open here, in Amber Falls. I missed my family and was ready to come home. I'll try it again when I'm ready."

"I just can't say the right thing, can I?" Sebastian asked.

"It's not that." Annabelle let her defenses fall. She was being hard on him, she knew it. "Writing a novel is very personal. You pour every ounce of yourself into it and rejection stings. You know this, you're in the business of rejection."

"I promise you this. I will read whatever you put in front of me."

His words surprised her. "You'd read my next novel?"

"You're a novelist now, are you?"

She could see a twinkle form in his eyes, not yet used to him joking with her and not berating her and she swatted his arm. "Obviously."

"Well, there are novelists, then there are *novelists*."

"I fail to see the difference between those words other than your inflection. A person who writes books writes books, end of story."

"You have a fair point. What's your favorite genre?"

"Whatever I want."

"Okaaaaay...what are you working on now?"

Oh, man, she didn't want to answer him, like she'd end up his punch line no matter what. But things were different now, and she didn't want to hold back this part of her.

"I'm writing a historical romance."

"I pictured you more of a contemporary writer."

She paused at this. What she wanted to yell was 'you rejected my last contemporary novel, you great big oaf' but what she said instead was, "I keep unfolding like a flower."

"The Regency era is very popular now. You'd have a good chance with that genre." He lay back on the bed, his hands behind his head. "Am I in the plot?"

"Why would you be in the plot?"

"I've heard your nicknames for me. My personal favorite was His-Royal-Pain-in-my-Ass."

Annabelle could feel her face warm. "I called you that ages ago, when you first got here."

"*Ages* ago," he teased. "A whole nine months."

"Besides, you weren't supposed to know that. It was a term of endearment, I swear."

Sebastian appeared thoughtful. "I can see that. It's very clear that you were hiding your ardor for me since we first met."

He had to be joking, but Annabelle's breath still caught. She wasn't sure he was wrong about that. It wasn't a secret that, even with the animosity between them, she sought him out, all the time. There was a connection between them that had been there since he'd come to Amber Falls. They'd been drawn to each other from the start.

She shifted, uncomfortable with her thoughts. "Do you want to know the plot?" she asked, wanting to shift the conversation.

"Of course I do."

"It's about this man—"

"A duke?"

"Obviously."

"Obviously," Sebastian parroted.

"It's about a duke who has had a lot of heartache in his life, loss, that he's not sure he can get over. He lost his family and his meddling mother wants him to remarry and he'll do anything to thwart her plans. He doesn't count on falling for the fake sweetheart he talks into fooling his mother."

Sebastian's eyes narrowed. "That sounds an awful lot like Wyatt Reed's real life."

"Can you blame me? Wanting to fix a person is primal. Besides, Wyatt Reed is just so dreamy, who wouldn't want to write a book about him?"

"Dreamy?"

Annabelle sighed. "Yep. The hair that's a touch too long, his permanent five o'clock shadow, the vulnerability he can't quite hide."

Sebastian pounced, and flipped Annabelle to her back, pinning her to the mattress.

"Has Wyatt Reed ever made you scream with pleasure?"

"To be fair, neither have you."

"You will, Annabelle. Before this night is over, I will make you scream."

Chapter Eighteen

Sebastian left Annabelle's in the early hours of the morning. She'd protested, but today was a big day for him, so he'd gone home and prepared for perhaps the most important thing he'd done in Amber Falls, so far. He found himself standing in front of the community center, holding a glass pie plate, with an incredulous Annabelle.

"This is why you left my bed this morning?" The confusion on her face was almost comical. "For pie?"

"Peach pie," was his explanation, and he motioned with his head for her to open the door.

"I gathered that." Annabelle walked with him to the judging table. "But why would you, of all the people in Amber Falls, make a peach pie?"

Sebastian set the pie down with satisfaction and was interrupted from answering by an approaching Mrs. Crenshaw.

"Hello, dear," she addressed Annabelle. "And Mr. Locke."

"Please, call me Sebastian," he offered.

He didn't know Mrs. Crenshaw well. She looked as old as the town itself, but there was a glimmer in her eyes that belied her age.

"Sebastian, then. Did I just see you put a pie on the judging table?" Her frail voice cracked, and he started to feel bad for wanting to win.

"You did. I thought I'd try my hand at this season's contest."

Mrs. Crenshaw was Amber Fall's reigning bake-off queen. She'd won fall's tater tot hotdish and winter's chili cook-off, and was clearly gearing up for another win.

Her voice grew stronger. "I'll have you know, I haven't lost a cook-off since Reagan was president."

Sebastian swallowed hard. Mrs. Crenshaw was still staring at him with a shrewd look, so obviously not the little old lady she had everyone fooled into believing. *So, this is how she's going to play it? I'm in.*

"It's a bake-off, not a cook-off," he shot back.

Mrs. Crenshaw's mouth pursed. "Call it what you want, that blue ribbon is mine."

"Not this time."

"Sorry, I got distracted by Devlin." Annabelle came back over to them. "You didn't tell me she was back in town."

"I'd better be going, they're going to start judging. Are you writing the article, Annabelle?" Mrs. Crenshaw continued at her nod, her feeble voice back. "I'll find you after so you can take a picture of me with my blue ribbon. Good luck, Sebastian."

Sebastian leaned in. "You're going down, Crenshaw," he whispered.

Mrs. Crenshaw broke into what could only be described as a cackle and walked away.

"That was strange," Annabelle noted as they found their seats.

"You've known her your whole life, and just now you're finding her strange?"

"Well, no," Annabelle admitted. "Here, let me sit on the outside so I can take pictures."

Sebastian lost his train of thought as they switched spots, Annabelle brushing against him and setting his body to high alert. He took off his suit jacket and draped it over his legs when he sat, hiding his arousal.

Annabelle nudged him, scooting closer, which did nothing to dampen his desire. "I asked you why you thought she was strange."

"For one, she claims she's won these things since the Reagan administration."

"Yeah, Prudence said the same thing after she lost the tater tot hotdish cook-off. She thought there might be something fishy going on. In fact"—she gestured to where the judging was taking place—"Joe is the head judge."

"What does that have to do with anything?"

She shot him a look. "I wrote an article on it in February for Valentine's Day?"

He shook his head.

"You proofread it for me?"

"Sorry, not ringing a bell."

Annabelle sighed. "Mrs. Crenshaw and Joe reconnected this winter after being apart for many years."

The lightbulb clicked. "Okay, yeah. The article was a great human-interest piece."

"Well, after that Prudence had the idea that Joe was rigging every contest so Mrs. Crenshaw would win. Maybe not rigging it, but trying to get noticed by her."

"That's quite the conspiracy theory."

"Pru said that there's no way one person could win every cooking contest without having some strings pulled." Annabelle snapped a picture of the mayor sampling Sebastian's pie. "Although there was a rumor going around when we were kids that she was a witch."

"That seems fitting, we are in Massachusetts," he joked.

"Back when Prudence, Grey and I were in fifth grade, we were practicing trick basketball shots at Grey's parents' and one of the shots broke a window in her house."

"That must've been one crazy shot. Isn't she across the street?"

"We were playing in the street. She came running out with a broom in her hand followed by her black cat, yelling at us. So, that didn't help the rumor mill. Turns out she's just a sweet old lady who had every right to be annoyed by a bunch of kids who broke her window."

"Sweet old lady?" The hair on the back of Sebatian's neck stood up. He turned around to see Agatha Crenshaw staring at him and he swallowed hard. "Witch or no, she can't win every time."

"Why are you so confident that you'll win? You didn't tell me you baked."

"I don't bake, I make peach pie."

Annabelle raised her eyebrows, clearly waiting for further explanation.

"I'm from Georgia, and if there's one thing I know, it's peaches."

"One thing you know?"

"Oh, I know a lot more than that, but as it pertains to this conversation, yes, I know peaches."

"I'm intrigued, tell me more about these peaches."

What he wanted to do was to relate peaches in an explicit way to the most delectable part of the female body, ripe and juicy, but he was in public and didn't need any more distractions in the form of Annabelle.

"My best friend's mom is a chef. She owns one of the best bakeries in Atlanta and when I heard about the peach pie contest, I asked her for a recipe. She did one better and we had Zoom calls where she went through it step by step."

Annabelle turned her full attention to him. "You're telling me that you sat at home video calling with your best friend's mom during your rare time off so you could learn how to bake a peach pie well enough to win a bake-off in Amber Falls?"

"I guess when you put it that way it doesn't seem—"

"That's so hot."

"What?" Sebastian started to sweat.

"Picturing you, at home while it's snowing out, baking pie after pie."

Annabelle slid her hand under his jacket and brushed his cock.

"Ripe, juicy peaches. Were they canned, or did you slice them fresh?"

He shifted in his seat, unable to stop the quiet groan that escaped his mouth, then he replied, "Fresh."

The sound of a clearing throat snapped him out of his daze and Annabelle snatched her hand back and fanned her face.

"Time to tally up the votes, folks," one of the judges called to the crowd.

Sebastian willed his erection to subside and, after a few deep breaths, he was under control.

"Are we sure this is correct?" The judge held a piece of folded paper and conferred with the others on the makeshift stage. They nodded, and he continued. "In a stunning upset, Sebastian Locke has won the blue ribbon in this year's peach pie bake-off."

A gasp rippled through the community center and a few scattered claps sounded. A flash went off as Annabelle took his picture.

"You seem surprised for someone who expected to win," she commented.

"I expected to win, I just didn't *expect* to win. This town has its own ecosystem, and I thought for sure that it wouldn't matter what I brought to the table."

"From the looks on everyone's faces, I think they thought that, too."

"Come on up, Mr. Locke." One judge motioned him forward.

As Sebastian made his way to the front of the room, pride swelled inside him. He'd won a contest that no out-of-towner had ever won, but that wasn't the reason for his feeling of fulfillment. After the initial shock of him winning, the crowd cheered with joy and happiness. They weren't upset that an outsider had come in and pulled the rug out from under the clear favorite. *Maybe an outsider didn't win.*

He got congratulations, claps on the back, handshakes and high-fives from everyone he passed. They knew him and he was surprised that he knew them. Mr. Skelton who ran the movie theater, Ms. Hathaway who had been the kindergarten teacher for the last fifty years, Mrs. Kincade who organized the walks for hunger to stock the food pantry when it was getting low. He wasn't the outsider he made himself out to be. He'd ingrained himself into Amber Falls — or maybe it had into him, he wasn't sure — but the sense of belonging was one that he hadn't ever felt, not even in his hometown of Atlanta.

Then there was Annabelle Winters. A strange peace settled over him when he thought of her. He knew, deep in his heart, that it wasn't the physical bond they shared that was making him so happy right now. He was happy just to be around her, even when they were at their worst, fighting like they'd never end.

Sebastian accepted the blue ribbon and held it up to the crowd. He scanned the faces beaming back at him, not one person begrudging this win. He realized that he'd had enough of the fake smiles in Atlanta, the hollow congratulations bestowed upon him while they plotted to one-up him next time, not knowing who wanted to take down the great Sebastian Locke. Reading a room was a strength of his and, with the clear exception of Mrs. Crenshaw, the people of Amber Falls had accepted him as one of their own.

Annabelle made her way to him, the crowd parting like the Red Sea. She stood a short distance away from him, her camera at the ready but not yet held up to take a picture. Sebastian's smile faltered for a moment, too aware of the fact that he could read this entire room of people, but he couldn't read *her*. He could never read her. From the moment she'd stepped into his office his first day in Amber Falls, it had been so clear to him that she was holding a piece of herself back from him. It irked him that he didn't know what this piece was and how he was desperate to find out.

"Let's see that blue ribbon, Mr. Locke," Annabelle said, back to business in the crowd of people.

Sebastian held the ribbon up while she snapped a few pictures. He felt the same sense of unease as he had earlier and turned his head to see Mrs. Crenshaw glaring daggers as she walked toward him. The Red Sea had crashed back into place, taking Annabelle away in a wave toward the next person to photograph, and he was now alone with Mrs. Crenshaw.

"So. You won the blue ribbon," she stated.

He glanced down at his ribbon. "It appears I did."

Her gaze narrowed and she leaned in.

"Don't ever let it happen again, Locke."

Sebastian was saved from having to reply when Joe materialized at Mrs. Crenshaw's side.

"Now, now, Agatha." Joe put a hand on her shoulder. "We can't win them all."

"Oh, dear, I was just telling Sebastian how happy I was to see the new people of this town taking these festivals so seriously. After all, it doesn't matter who wins as long as we're having fun."

Sebastian's eyes almost rolled out of his head at her statement, but he could play along with the best of them.

"Yes, Mrs. Crenshaw said she was happy she finally lost, especially to such a handsome and accomplished young man."

"Well," Mrs. Crenshaw tittered back, "young is a relative term for you, dear, let's not go too far."

There was a beat of silence before Joe started to lead Mrs. Crenshaw away.

"Let's go see what the soup of the day is at Finnegan's, Agatha. I'm ready for some lunch."

"Of course, dear. I'm cold and could use some good warm soup."

Sebastian let go of the fact that she was wearing a turtleneck in the middle of their summer heat wave, but did a double take when she reached up to adjust her neckline. To a casual observer she could've been straightening it out, but to Sebastian, who had been watching her closely, she made a clear slashing motion across her throat.

Annabelle had just reappeared at his side in time to catch the motion.

"Um, were you just cursed by Mrs. Crenshaw?"

"No, she's just an old lady who is too set in her ways."

"I'm sorry to break it to you, but you were definitely cursed. We have to go sage your house. How much salt do you have a home?"

"How much salt? I have the normal amount of salt."

Annabelle shook her head. "Not enough, we need to buy it in bulk."

"You're joking, right? You just got done saying that she wasn't a witch."

"I was trying to make you feel better. I never joke about Mrs. Crenshaw's curses."

Sebastian was over it. He'd won the contest, beat Mrs. Crenshaw and had taken pictures for the newspaper article tomorrow. All he wanted to do now was to get Annabelle alone.

"Don't you need a quote from the big winner for your article?" He steered her toward the closed-up kitchen in the back of the room. He pushed his back against the door, thankful that it opened, and clicked the lock closed once they were through.

"I do, but I figured that we could do that later." Annabelle noticed where they were, and her nose scrunched in clear confusion. "What are we doing in the community center kitchen?"

"It was the closest room that I could lock behind us."

"Why would you need to lock—"

Her words were cut off as Sebastian pulled her against him, his hands greedily seeking to undo her bound hair.

"Don't be dense, Annabelle." He pressed his mouth to hers.

He kissed her softly, softer than he'd anticipated considering the arousal rolling through him. She sighed and opened up to him, her tongue pulling his in.

Sebastian had denied himself of her for what seemed like an eternity, even though it had only been nine months. There was no reason anymore to keep himself from her, and he didn't want to. He'd opened Annabelle's Pandora's box and their mutual lust had been released, but he was searching for the hope still locked inside. If hope came to him in the form of Annabelle's body, he'd be glad to take it.

He trailed his lips down her neck. "I couldn't wait."

"I hope this kitchen is clean."

"Oh, God, if you're worrying about a clean kitchen right now, I'm not doing my job."

Annabelle fumbled with the closure of his pants and unzipped it, reaching in to grasp his cock. Sebastian pushed into her hand, back and forth, letting the friction harden him even more.

"You'd be surprised at how dirty it can be," she breathed, seeking out his mouth again as she pumped his cock.

"You'd be surprised at how dirty *I* can be," he promised, pulling away from her and turning her back to him.

Sebastian placed her hands on a gleaming stainless-steel countertop, moving her so she was leaning on her elbows. He rocked into her from behind, moving her skirt up a little higher with each motion. He almost came when he saw that she wasn't wearing any panties.

"You've been walking around with no underwear on?"

"I just don't see the point."

"Fuck me, neither do I."

After rolling on a condom, he pushed into her with a smooth motion, the tightness of her cunt from this angle squeezed him so that his cock made a *pop* sound when he pulled out of her. He grabbed her ass and spread her open, watching himself go in and out of her as he fucked her from behind.

A tension started in his chest that had nothing to do with his building orgasm. Only days had passed since they'd first gotten together and he already felt too connected to her, too needy in her presence, pulled into her orbit and forced to stay as close to her as he could. *It was too much, too soon.*

He pushed this niggling thought aside and forced himself to focus on the pure physical pleasure he got from Annabelle. Her skin was smooth, with a slight tan on her arms and legs but pure white on her bottom. The dusky pink of her core, pulling him into her over and over again. The smell of sex and arousal and her, filling their space. Her hair unbound and free, silky in his hands. Each of these overwhelmed him, though, and he wasn't going to win any awards today for finesse or stamina. He needed to finish in her and he needed to do it now.

Sebastian grabbed her hips, pulling her back into him, their skin clapping together in a sensual rhythm, and he reached around to circle her clit with his finger.

"Right there, Sebastian, don't stop," Annabelle begged.

He didn't. He couldn't. He wouldn't.

He collapsed over her back as he buried his cock in her with one final thrust, continuing to touch her clit until she gripped him with her own orgasm, milking even more pleasure out of him than he thought possible.

"Well, fuck," he heard Annabelle mutter, her head on her arms.

Sebastian stood and put her skirt to rights, after pulling out of her and taking off the condom, lifting her up from the table and into his arms.

"You need to win more bake-offs, if that's how you react to winning." She laid her head on his chest.

"That's not reacting to winning, that's all for you," he admitted.

Sebastian felt her stiffen and he mentally kicked himself for letting the words slip out. He didn't loosen his arms, though, didn't want her to pull away from him.

He had his own hangups about relationships—the end with Serena had done a number on him—but he didn't want to pressure Annabelle into anything that she wasn't ready for, or something more than what this was. So, he pulled away when he wanted to keep holding her.

"Let's head out, I've got some adoring fans out there who I'm sure want a chance to talk with me about my winning pie."

Annabelle rolled her eyes. "If you can call a bunch of octogenarians adoring fans, go ahead."

That was better, much more like herself. He'd have to watch it from now on. If he interpreted her reaction right, he was moving too fast. He didn't want to appear needy or clingy, no one wanted that.

Chapter Nineteen

Annabelle lay in an unfamiliar bed the next morning.

She'd woken up alone to the dawn, light just peeking through the curtains on the window that overlooked the lake, the sun's rays starting to bounce off the water. She flipped her pillow over, hoping the other side was cooler, the open window not doing any good other than letting in humid air that was far too hot for the time of day.

She was restless without Sebastian, not sure what to do alone in his house. He'd told her before they fell asleep in the early morning hours that he ran almost every morning, if he was gone when she awoke. If anything, the silence was what had jarred her out of a peaceful sleep. Amber Falls wasn't a bustling metropolis by any means, but her downtown condo *was* on one of the main streets and she couldn't get away from the sounds of the town waking up.

This morning there were no garbage trucks, car engines or train whistles—nothing that lulled her back to sleep on a usual day. A few birds chirped and the trees rustled in the heavy air, but that was all. The silence outside was no match for the noise inside her head, though.

When she was with Sebastian, she was able to push the strangeness aside. Being physical with Sebastian felt normal—their bodies fit together like they were each other's half. But when they were together physically, they didn't have to talk. It was everything outside of that she was struggling with. The last few weeks had chipped away at a little bit of this, getting to know him and how he operated, but the last vestiges of unfamiliarity were still lingering, and were a loud voice in her head. Being alone in his house amplified this noise.

Annabelle had been here before, only a few weeks ago when she was helping Sebastian prepare for Sofia's arrival. Then, she'd had her loathing to fall back on. She hadn't cared that he had a prominent display of family pictures on his fireplace mantle—pictures with his sister, his whole family, smiling and clearly enjoying their togetherness.

Back then she hadn't noticed the color of the throw blanket draped over his chair. Now, she wondered if the air conditioning was too cool for him, or the lake air blew into the living room while he was watching TV and he needed to cover up. Did he like comedies or dramas? Did he prefer television shows or movies? The thoughts overwhelmed her for a moment and she took a deep breath to dispel her unease. This relationship didn't have any higher stakes than any other. They were just having fun.

Liar.

Annabelle trailed a finger over the blanket and imagined it smelled like him. She was ready to prove her theory correct when she heard the front door open. She pulled her hand back like he was going to catch her going through his drawers, then laughed at her own foolishness.

"Hey, Winters, I thought you'd still be sleeping."

Sebastian hadn't broken his habit of calling her Winters yet, and she wasn't sad about it. Something about that name coming from his lips made her excited.

"No, I couldn't sleep, it's too hot out."

Sebastian lifted the hem of his shirt and wiped his face, nodding in agreement.

"You're not lying. It's not even July yet and the humidity is killing me."

"Why would you get up so early to go out? I wouldn't be in such a hurry to leave bed when the sun came up."

"I had to work off all that pie I ate yesterday." Sebastian quirked a smile, the insufferable man.

"Was it at least a good run?"

Sebastian wiped his face again then took off his shirt, apparently giving up on the sweat.

"It was stimulating."

"Stimulating, you say?" Annabelle walked over to where Sebastian stood. Her need to be close to him was almost alarming.

"Running gives me energy." He reached his hands up and braced them on the doorframe, stretching his lean body.

"I think I'd be exhausted after."

"No, just the opposite. Every drop of blood in me is rushing through my body and I feel alive."

Annabelle blew a stream of air onto a bead of sweat that formed on his chest and was promising to caress its way down his body. She watched as it started to trail over his chest, to his taut abs and down the trail of hair into his shorts. She lifted her finger and followed the path it had taken, hooking it in his waistband.

"It seems to me that all your blood is rushing to one place right now."

Sebastian inhaled as she pulled his shorts down, letting his erection jut out.

"That's personally my most favorite place ever."

"How eloquent."

"What can I say? You're in my shirt, in my house with your hand around my cock. Eloquence isn't the first thing on my mind."

Annabelle led him to the couch and pushed him down.

"I'll show you how eloquent I can make this."

* * * *

A week had passed and Annabelle was getting used to being out at Sebastian's. The silence calmed her, centered her, and rejuvenated her. The few days she had spent alone in her condo were lonely and loud.

As it was, the crunch of their sneakers on the gravel road was the only sound aside from the lowing of cows.

"I can't believe you talked me into running with you," Annabelle wheezed.

"That's so cute, you think this is running."

"How is it not? I have shin splints!"

"No, you don't, Annabelle. You should've stretched more this morning."

"You didn't give me time. You practically threw my shoes at me and said, 'today's the day, Winters,'" she imitated his deep baritone.

Sebastian shrugged. "It's about time you figured out the joys of country running."

Annabelle's ponytail swished back and forth as they moved. Running wasn't that bad. She was in great shape, not from her little-used gym membership, but from living within walking distance from most places downtown. Plus, you *had* to be in shape to walk everywhere in stilettos.

"How is country running different than city running?" she asked.

Crunch, crunch, crunch.

They'd moved some distance forward before he answered.

"A lot like how the country is different than the city." He glanced over at her. "You should know, you've lived in both."

"Yes and no," Annabelle admitted. "The city limits of Amber Falls aren't exactly the country like it is out here. This is Hicksville compared to Atlanta, but it's not the same. I've never lived out here."

"Fair enough."

"Are you going to answer my question?"

"Well, the air for one. The humidity in Atlanta was stifling and unforgiving. Even in the winter I thought there was a heaviness to it that never went away."

Annabelle couldn't help but inhale the sweet smell of country air. "You're right. It was oppressive. The air out here is way different than in town, even. It smells like corn, animals and hay. It's not a combination that I thought would be appealing in the least, but I've come to like it."

"Here you can breathe free, even on the muggiest day."

She glanced over at him, hearing a note of bitterness in his voice and saw the grim set of his mouth. Interesting. She felt that Sebastian wasn't just here to run a newspaper, but that he was on some sort of self-imposed isolation.

"Did you have friends you ran with in Atlanta?"

His gaze shuttered and Annabelle thought she'd touched a raw nerve with the mention of friends.

"I ran in Atlanta."

Annabelle knew she should leave it alone, that he was clearly avoiding her question, but she wanted to peel back the layers of Sebastian Locke and see what made him tick. The more time they spent together, the more she became fascinated by the way his mind worked and she was willing to get a bit dirty to find out more.

"Well, yes, I gathered that." She tried not to sound impatient—he would surely clam up if she did. "I'm curious if you like running with a group, or do you prefer by yourself?"

"It's been a solo interest of mine."

"I'm flattered that you begged me to come with you this morning, then."

"Wait, you said earlier that I demanded you come with. I believe you even claimed I threw shoes at you."

Annabelle shrugged. "I can frame it however I want, considering I'm out here when it's eighty degrees at seven am."

Sebastian smiled, back to himself again. "Look at you holding a conversation while running and not being winded."

"Ha! You admit we're running."

"All right, I'll give it to you, we're running."

A few minutes later, a stitch was starting to form in her side.

"As much fun as I'm having, are we almost done?"

"Yeah, let's take this shortcut around the lake. We'll be home twice as fast."

Their strides ate up the short distance, but Annabelle was very overheated.

"I need to shower. I'm about ten degrees too hot right now."

"Why shower when you have a whole lake at your disposal?" He gestured for her to follow him around the back of the house.

"I don't think so, I have no interest in jumping into a lake this early. I'll just run in and shower."

"Are you chicken?"

"Of what, swimming in a lake?"

"Not everyone likes to."

Annabelle studied the dark surface. "Lakes don't bother me."

"Good." Sebastian dove forward, skimming the surface of the water and rose up about ten feet out. He shook his head, his hair spraying water all around him, like a golden retriever.

"The water is perfect. I guarantee you won't regret cooling off."

"What the hell, right?" Annabelle was so hot from running she thought she might pass out if she didn't get some relief. She toed off her shoes and took one step into the water, then a few more until she was waist deep. Still, she didn't have enough relief from the heat, so she did what Sebastian had done and dove into the shallow water, making sure she kept toward the surface.

"This is amazing." She'd swum out far enough that she had to tread water and dunked herself back under, holding her breath until the coolness of the water soothed her hot skin.

When she surfaced, she noticed Sebastian staring at her.

"What?" she asked.

"You're beautiful, you know that?"

Her heart skipped a beat, then started pounding double time.

"I have to look like a drowned rat."

Sebastian moved closer to her. She was still treading water, but he was tall enough to stand.

"You don't."

He reached out and pulled her into his arms and the water between them whooshed away as she came flush to his chest. She wrapped her legs around him, and he ran his hands down to her bottom, moving against her.

"Did I tell you that running invigorates me?"

"You said it was stimulating." She tightened her legs around him. His erection was heavy and hard. "But now that you mention it, you do seem very invigorated."

Sebastian lowered his mouth to hers and she opened for him without hesitation. Her senses were being overwhelmed—hot skin, cold water, sexy man.

Annabelle found out with Sebastian that kissing was a lost art. The rush to get to copulation often bypassed one of the most arousing things two people could do, the building of tension that could only be released one way. She could kiss Sebastian all day because, damn, he was good at it. The languorous slide of his tongue against hers, the perfect rhythm of sucking and pulling then sweeping into her mouth, the co-mingling of breaths. Yes, he was a master at this and she was only too happy to be his servant. But the day ahead would be busy and she needed to get ready.

"Sebastian, I have to go."

"No," he whispered out the word between kisses.

"I'm meeting the mayor at eight and I need to get ready."

"You owe me one after I bailed you out of that bad date."

"Thanks for reminding me of that trainwreck."

"I'll be quick."

Annabelle loosened her legs and swam toward shore, avoiding his attempt to capture her.

"Ah, the words every girl can't wait to hear. 'I'll be quick'."

"You know what I mean, Winters."

Annabelle shook what water she could off her, grabbed her shoes and walked to the house.

"Did you know you call me Winters, still, when you get upset?" She turned to see him close behind her.

"I'm not upset. I was in the middle of a perfectly good make-out session when you decided you had to go." He held the door for her and motioned her onto the screened-in porch, a devilish glint popping up in his eyes. "Clothes off out here. I'm not going to let you traipse through my house dripping water everywhere. Those floors are reclaimed two-hundred-year-old barn wood."

"This is oak flooring from the 1950s if it's a day."

She lost her train of thought when Sebastian started stripping. First he tossed his tight white shirt onto the floor and his running shorts joined the pile a moment later. He stood there, grinning, his cock now free and looking so good.

Fuck. She was in trouble.

"Even so, clothes off," he repeated.

The thought crossed Annabelle's mind to ignore him and go inside, but to be honest, the mayor could wait, and she didn't want to.

Her clothes were harder to get off than his, they were tight and wet and any thoughts she had to make this part sexy went out the window at her struggle.

"You could help me, you know."

"I'm having far too much fun watching. Keep doing those little jumps, I'm enjoying watching your breasts."

Annabelle pulled off her sports bra with a final tug and threw it at him. "These breasts?" She pointed to them, pert and round with nipples pebbled hard from the cool air on the porch and walked toward him.

Sebastian swallowed hard. "Those are the ones."

"I'm going to ask that you stop ogling and start touching, sir."

He lowered his mouth, capturing one nipple between his teeth and giving a slight tug. Liquid fire shot through her at the contact and she ran her hands through his wet hair, holding him to her. He laved a tongue over the stiff peak, alternating sucking and nipping until she guided him to the other breast and he repeated his movements.

She threw her head back and let the pleasure roll through her, not protesting when he lowered her to the floor and welcoming his weight as he settled over her. He stilled, the tip of his cock at her entrance, nudging slightly, teasing her.

"Wait." He reached into his running shorts, took out a condom and put it on.

"Only you would bring condoms on a run."

"If a man doesn't have hope, he doesn't have anything."

Annabelle held his gaze as he was poised over her, waiting for the first thrust, when his eyes softened. He kissed her lips, a gentle caress. Then her nose and forehead. Her heart squeezed at the emotion he was showing her. The tenderness she felt for Sebastian in this moment left her unable to breathe.

They butted heads so much that seeing him this way was still a jarring experience. Despite her wanting to get to know the man behind the empire, he was still an enigma to her, holding back a crucial part of him that me might never show her. She had to accept this and take him for who he was.

Even with this, she was seeing a different side to him, one that became clearer every day. The man in Atlanta, hell, even the man that showed up in Amber Falls, wasn't the same one that was on top of her now. The man on top of her held her hand as they walked down the street. He opened her car door for her and made sure she'd had enough to eat before finishing off dinner. He shared the covers with her, snored only slightly and let her get into the bathroom first in the morning. He wasn't the man who kicked her out of his office, and she realized that love might have something to do with this. At least on her part.

The fact that she came to this realization while lying on the hard floor of a screened-in porch with him still poised over her didn't lessen it at all. She tried to peek into his soul, to search his eyes to see if any of her affection was reflected to her, but she only saw dark pools of desire. This wasn't the time or place to declare love, if that's even what it was.

When he pushed into her, she moaned at the pleasure and her head dropped back to the floor.

"That feels so good, you have no idea," she pulled him closer, her mouth opening hungrily for him, his tongue moving with the same rhythm as his cock.

He braced his arms and lifted himself up.

"I have some idea."

Sebastian reached under her and grabbed her butt, angling her so he hit the spot deep inside her, the one that melted her to a pool of lava.

Annabelle braced her feet on the floor, pushing herself up, meeting him thrust for thrust. They were battling, whether either of them wanted to admit it, or whether either of them knew what for. She let him drive into her, wanting to flip the script and take control, but she sensed a need in him that she didn't want to control, different from when they'd first made love.

Maybe it was like he'd said earlier, after the run, that his body was so tuned up with adrenaline and the blood flowing that he was unstoppable, relentless in his pursuit of pleasure. She was so focused on Sebastian that her orgasm took her by surprise. She shouted out, her release so intense that she saw flashes of light in the periphery of her vision, but he didn't stop. He changed the angle, relentless in his pounding. He was winning this battle, but she wasn't going to let him have all the fun.

Annabelle reached down and touched her clit, so sensitive from her intense orgasm.

"Oh, fuck, yes," Sebastian panted. "Touch yourself for me."

She screwed her eyes shut, forcing all thoughts out of her head other than those of pleasure and release.

Her singular focus was on coming again, and if she happened to brush his cock with her fingers each time he entered her, then that was a bonus. She clenched her muscles and squeezed and did what she knew now her body was made for, to give him pleasure. Her second orgasm overtook her and he pumped into her and held himself, spilling his seed. She shuddered with each wave of pleasure and strained up to him, trying to take him deeper into her, even though he was grinding in as far as he could go.

Finally, she unclenched her body as he collapsed on her. They were hot and sweaty again, like they hadn't cooled down at all in the lake, breathing like they'd just finished running.

"Holy fuck, Winters."

"Mmmhmmm." The reply wasn't articulate, but it would have to do.

"I can't move, I'm sorry if I'm too heavy."

On the contrary, the weight of him on her was almost as pleasurable as her two orgasms. That she could be his cushion and he could rest his weary self on someone, her specifically, in a post-coital vulnerability. Annabelle put her arms around him and squeezed, trying to absorb whatever negativity she could.

Sebastian rolled onto his side, groaning as he went, and took off the condom.

"Don't get old," he stated.

"I don't think age has as much to do with it as the hard floor."

"Even so, that's free advice for you."

Annabelle sat, stretched her arms upward, then lay on his chest and snuggled close to him.

"Have you ever played hooky?" she asked.

"I thought you had a big interview with the mayor today?"

"I do, but I can postpone."

Sebastian stroked her hair. "You know, I don't think I've ever not gone to work unless I was sick."

Annabelle popped up and propped an arm on his chest.

"Let's do it, then. You and me, call in sick to work and see where the day takes us."

"You know I'm your boss still, right?"

"Then we won't get in trouble."

She watched him as he contemplated this. His dark eyebrows furrowed, and she noticed the smudges of exhaustion under his eyes. She now knew he was a fitful sleeper, often up late working, then back to it in the early morning, only to have the precious little time in between interrupted by calls and texts. Everyone needed him.

"When was the last time you napped?"

"Napped?" he repeated.

"Yes, you know when you close your eyes during the day and go to sleep. It's glorious when you don't have to do anything and can drift off, no alarm set, no hoping that morning won't come too soon."

"I'm an adult, I don't nap. Besides, it's still morning."

"Then all the better to get back into bed, turn the air conditioning on full blast and burrow under the covers until we can't sleep anymore."

Sebastian closed his eyes for a moment then nodded.

"I can't think of anything I'd rather do than nap with you, Winters."

Chapter Twenty

Sebastian felt refreshed. He wasn't sold on the idea of napping, rather the thought of spending the day in bed with Annabelle is what had the appeal, but when they'd gotten back into bed and his head hit the pillow, he was a convert. The morning passed in blissful slumber, tangled in his little cocoon of Annabelle.

"Morning."

"It's afternoon," Annabelle grumbled.

"You're not a ray of sunshine, even when it's not morning, are you?"

"No, I like my sleep. It's hard to get up."

Sebastian stretched, conscious of her naked form next to him, and his body stirred. When he'd told her earlier this morning that she was gorgeous, he'd meant it. Nothing was more beautiful to him than a woman disheveled from lovemaking and if he'd ever thought that he'd seen this kind of beauty before he was so mistaken. Nothing in his whole life compared to Annabelle Winters. Naked, with a leg thrown over him, she looked up at him, her hair a wild mess, no makeup on and with still-sleepy eyes, he stopped breathing.

He touched her hair. He'd found out that he liked running his hands through it and got frustrated when she had it up. When it was down, like now, it beckoned to him, and he gave in. Her eyebrows were raised and he realized he'd missed a question.

"I'm sorry, what?"

"I asked what you wanted to do on the rest of our day of playing hooky?"

He thought for a moment, which was a moment longer than he needed.

"I want to stay in bed with you and see how many times I can make you come."

"Absolutely not."

"I see no reason why that shouldn't be my goal for today."

Annabelle laughed and pushed away from him, appearing to be in deep thought.

"Tell you what—if we get out and do something this afternoon, I promise you that you can have your way with me tonight."

Sebastian pulled her on top of him so she straddled his middle, the cheeks of her ass nestling his hard cock. He undulated his hips, letting his cock slide up and down.

"That's not good enough, Winters."

Annabelle rocked on him, her clit brushing his abdomen with every forward movement. Her eyes became unfocused and took the truth out of her next words.

"It's going to have to be."

"I don't think so," he insisted, bringing his hands up to cup her breasts. He'd play this game with her as long as she wanted, but he wasn't going to make it a fair playing field.

Annabelle loved it when he touched her breasts. There was a direct connection from her nipples to her clit and the more he touched her up here, the wetter she got down there. A gentle pinch made her groan and with a harder one, her wetness spread. He wanted that wetness all over him and moved one hand to reposition her over him, not quite ready to take her. She slid forward and back still, but this time his hard cock was nestled in her seam, all that glorious nectar spreading up and down his erection and he nudged her clit with each thrust.

He watched her as she moved, her breasts forgotten for now. Annabelle's hair was swaying with her, brushing over his own chest with her movements, heightening his need to take her. But not yet. He wanted her to make herself come like this, so uninhibited. Her arms were braced on either side of his head, her eyes closed. Sebastian loved how she focused on her orgasm, and this deepened his own desire. He wanted to see her come, to see her face when she found her pleasure and made himself not reach out to touch her, to let her find her release on her own terms and not his.

Sebastian didn't rock his hips or move with her, and when she put the condom on and let him slip into her, the restraint of stillness built up his orgasm to a peak he'd never experienced before. Sensation and no action. He was at Annabelle's mercy and would come when she let him. When she finally spasmed, rocking to prolong her release, her inner muscles gripped him like the warmest fist and he came harder than he ever had, motionless and spilling into her.

He knew now why an orgasm was described as *la petite mort*. His soul left his body and was only coaxed back by Annabelle's kiss on his lips.

"Okay, now we can go do something," she whispered.

The rest of the day took them on a ramble about the Amber Falls countryside. They stopped at garage sales and fruit and vegetable stands then at a flea market on their way back into town.

"Oh, please?" Annabelle begged him. "I've always wanted an antique chest for the end of my bed that I can put blankets in. I know I said the last garage sale was the *last one*, but I mean it this time."

Sebastian pretended to think it over. The truth was, he didn't want this day to end. From the morning run, to their napping and lovemaking, it had so far been everything he thought a perfect day with Annabelle would be. It also didn't escape him that he'd turned off his cellphone and didn't care what he could be missing.

"Of course we can."

Annabelle squealed. "Yes!"

"If I'd known you would get that excited over an antique chest, I would've been looking for one all day."

He parked the car in the dusty makeshift parking lot and walked around to open her door for her.

"I have a very specific idea of what I want." She grabbed his hand as they walked through the lot to the first row of canopies and tents.

"Tell me and I'll keep an eye out for it."

"Well, when I say I have a very specific idea, I mean I'll know it when I see it."

"That's as clear as mud," he teased.

They wandered for a while and made small talk with locals.

"Do you miss it?" Annabelle asked.

"What?"

"Georgia." She gestured to the crowd. "This is the complete opposite of what your life was not even a year ago."

Sebastian shrugged, putting off answering. The question was loaded. Did he miss the overcrowding and crime? No. Did he miss being able to get a plate of sushi at midnight, hell, at all? Yes. He was saved from having to answer when he spotted a woman he'd seen a few times sneak up on them.

"Don't look now, but a small woman dressed in heels and a suit has been following us for a while now. I think she thinks she's being covert, but she's clearly staring at us."

"I know you're quite the specimen of a man, but women are following you now?"

"I didn't say me, I said us."

"Well, where is this superspy?" Annabelle scanned the crowd. "Mom?"

"Annabelle, sweetie! I stopped by the office today since you didn't answer your cell and Mrs. Johnson told me you were out sick." The woman took in Sebastian standing next to Annabelle, holding her hand. "I see."

Annabelle dropped Sebastian's hand like a hot potato. "It's not what you think, Mom."

Sebastian blinked hard at this statement. It shouldn't bug him that he was meeting Annabelle's mom for the first time and she was downplaying their acquaintance. If you put aside the fact that he was a total catch, the reality was that that they'd only been sleeping together, with no labels, so her words could make sense.

"I'm LuAnne Winters, Annabelle's mom." She extended her hand. "You're the one who broke her heart."

"Mom!"

"Well, he did a real number on you." She took her hand back, clearly rescinding her offer of a handshake.

"He did not, he rejected a book, that's all."

LuAnne's eyes narrowed at Sebastian, but her words were directed at Annabelle. "Did you at least get him to read another one of your books?"

Sebastian looked at Annabelle. "What does she mean?"

"Nothing. She means nothing."

He felt a stab low in his gut. He didn't want to, he truly didn't want to, but flashbacks of Serena went through his mind. He picked her up and moved her back into the cobwebbed part of his brain, where she belonged.

"LuAnne!" a voice from behind him hollered.

"Oh, thank God." Annabelle turned. "Shirley, I'm so glad you're here."

Sebastian spotted a tall redhead with bouncing curls bounding up to them. She was the spitting image of Prudence, with a few years tacked on.

"Sebastian, this is Prudence's mom, Shirley. Shirley, Sebastian Locke," Annabelle made the introductions.

To Annabelle's apparent surprise and LuAnne's clear annoyance, Sebastian reached out and pulled Shirley into a hug.

"Shirley, how have you been?"

"You two know each other?" LuAnne look about ready to explode at this revelation.

"We met this spring at Prudence and Greyson's house," Shirley explained. "How is the remodeling coming?"

"I'm done with what I need to do." He nodded to Annabelle. "Annabelle helped me finish it off last month."

LuAnne's eyebrows rose. "You've been out to his house?"

"Mom."

Annabelle shot a pleading look at Sebastian, but he had no clue what to say. The energy between mother and daughter was uncomfortable.

"Mom, we can talk about this later."

Shirley turned to LuAnne and said accusingly, "I told you to leave them alone. They don't need your interference."

"*Moi*?" LuAnne touched her chest. "I would never interfere. I was just taking an interest in my daughter's life."

"I'm sorry," Shirley spoke to Annabelle. "We saw you an hour ago and I've been physically stopping her from accosting you until she gave me the slip."

"Accosting?" LuAnne scoffed. "Since when is talking to my daughter —"

"Mom," Annabelle interrupted her. "It was nice to see you, but we're doing some shopping right now."

LuAnne's eyes glinted. "Oh, really? Are you shopping around the Regency Romance you're writing?"

"Aaaaand this is when we leave." Shirley grabbed LuAnne and marched her away.

LuAnne didn't leave without a fight, calling as she went, "Don't forget your father's birthday coming up, he likes civil war memorabilia. You can bring a plus one! You didn't tell me you'd met Sebastian Locke, Shirley."

Sebastian watched the women go, his head spinning at the speed of their conversation, only minutes had passed, but it seemed like they'd recited *War and Peace*.

"Wow, they're quite the..." He wasn't sure how to end the sentence without insulting Annabelle's mother, so he didn't.

"Parental periscope? Yeah." Annabelle sighed.

"She sounded pretty upset. What did you tell her about Atlanta?"

"Just what happened. I pitched a book and you rejected it."

"She sure made it sound like a lot more than that."

"You know moms. You can't tell me that yours never stood up for you in a super embarrassing way?"

Sebastian didn't want to let this go quite yet—he didn't like the way LuAnne talked to him—but he knew Annabelle was deflecting the conversation and he let her. For now.

"I was in my first year of college and I got a C in some middle management class I was taking to get credits. She was so cool when I told her, but the next day she called my professor and told him off. She said that I'd been studying under one of the greatest CEOs of all time and he needed to get his head out of his ass if he thought I was only C material."

"Was the grade justified?"

"Oh yes. I slacked off in that class because I thought I already knew all I needed."

"You see? Parents don't always know everything."

Sebastian left the conversation at that and they wandered through the flea market for a while longer. His fingers twitched with the need to hold her hand again. Their hands brushed occasionally, but neither grasped the other. He wasn't sure what had changed, but he felt stuffy and uncomfortable, like his shirt was too tight at the collar. He shifted, trying to ease his unease, but it followed them down the pathways and stilted their conversation.

They'd discussed Annabelle's writing and her book before, and he'd been serious when he'd told her he'd like to read it, but they'd talked about her book more than once over the last few weeks and now her mom was asking about it? It didn't sit well with him.

"Well, Sebastian Locke," a cultured voice sounded from behind them. "This is the last place I would've expected to find you."

They both turned and Sebastian had trouble putting a name to the woman standing there.

"Hi. I'm sorry, I don't recall your name."

"Silly, you know my name. I did rock your world, after all." She turned to Annabelle and winked. "I'm Brenda."

Sebastian's hackles went up. He hadn't had any time since he moved to Amber Falls for extracurricular activities like she was hinting, and he recalled that he'd only met her once.

"We had dinner with a group last fall. I haven't seen you since then." His voice was cold enough to ice over the Caribbean Sea.

"I beat you at pool? You said you never lost and were very impressed."

He had a vague memory of that night, but he was raised a gentleman and had better manners than to tell her how forgettable she was.

"This is Annabelle Winters." He paused, not sure how to continue. "One of my reporters at the newspaper."

He knew he'd made a mistake as soon as Annabelle's eyebrows shot up at this.

"You're out here doing a story, then?"

"Yeah, something like that."

Annabelle stiffened at the words he'd thrown out so casually. It wasn't a tit for tat—he wasn't that petty—but he didn't know how to introduce her after the run in with her mom. This seemed like the safest bet, all things considered.

"Okay, well." Brenda waited for Sebastian to continue the conversation and backed away when he didn't. "I'll see you around."

Neither moved after Brenda walked away.

"I think we've seen everything we can here." Annabelle avoided his eyes. "You ready to head out?"

"Annabelle, I don't know anything about that woman other than she was with a group of people I was with one night after I moved here. Nothing happened."

"I'm just your employee, sir. Don't worry about me."

"You know that's not how I meant it."

Annabelle sighed. "I have a lot to do at home that I've pushed off this last week. Can you drop me off?"

Sebastian couldn't think of anything to say, so they left.

They drove in silence on the way back to town, the sound of the radio the only thing keeping it from becoming unbearably awkward. When he pulled up in front of her condo, he'd thought of ten different ways to apologize, or at least start another conversation about it, but she hopped out as soon as he stopped, then poked her head back in.

"I'll call you, okay?"

She didn't wait for an answer and slammed the door, then was gone, and Sebastian was alone and at a loss of what to do now. The thought of going home to an empty house didn't appeal to him in the least, and as he eased back into the road he decided to stop for a drink. When he pulled up to Finnegan's and saw the packed bar, his energy left him. He was about to pull away when he saw a shadow in the other building Gabe owned, next to Finnegan's. He got out of the car seeing Gabe through the glass, he waved. Gabe smiled motioning to the front door, opening it a few moments later.

"Hey, I'm just working on some shelves, wanna come in?"

"Thanks, man, I'd love to. I was going to stop for a drink, but I didn't think I could face a crowd."

Gabe walked over to a makeshift table made by a plank of wood and two sawhorses and picked up a bottle.

"I've got some whiskey, if you want?" He gestured to a mini fridge. "Or a beer?"

"A cold beer sounds great right now."

"What's on your mind?" Gabe asked after they sat in two folding chairs and cracked their drinks.

"How can you tell something's on my mind?"

Gabe shrugged. "Experience. I've tended bar for a long time."

Sebastian took a long swig of his beer. "It's Winters. We seem to have hit a snag."

"I thought things were going well between you two."

"'The course of true love never did run smooth'," he quoted.

Gabe sputtered on his drink. "I'm sorry, what?"

"Love in the figurative sense, of course," Sebastian tried to assure him, but he felt a kick in the ribs at this denial. *Fuck.* This was way more complicated than he thought.

"Okay," Gabe drawled out. "Tell me what happened."

This wasn't a place he liked to frequent — so used to being used that he was second guessing what had happened these last few days. Sebastian didn't know where to start, so he picked the beginning.

"I'm sure someone somewhere along the way told you about my old girlfriend, Serena?"

"Devlin has kept me appraised of your past."

"Gotta love small towns." He continued when Gabe just shrugged. "I thought for sure she was the one. We were together for a long time, and when I asked her to marry me, she all but laughed in my face."

"Sebastian, that sucks."

"I was *so sure* about my decision and I would've bet my entire fortune on her saying yes. And I was wrong." He looked at Gabe. "I'm never wrong."

"Whatever has happened in your past, you need to leave it there. You're not wrong about Annabelle. She doesn't have a duplicitous bone in her body."

"It's more than that. We ran into her mom today at a flea market outside town and she not only accused me of breaking Annabelle's heart, she then made it sound like Annabelle was supposed pitch me another novel, but then invited me to her dad's birthday party. My head is spinning, and this all is moving too fast."

Gabe whistled. "LuAnne is a handful on her best day, I wouldn't take anything she said to heart."

"Well, then we ran into an old acquaintance of mine after and Annabelle seemed upset that I didn't introduce her as more than an employee."

"C'mon, that sounds bad no matter how you put it. You're sleeping with her and you introduce her as your employee?"

Sebastian ran a hand through his hair. "But she didn't introduce me at *all* to her mom. LuAnne had to introduce herself, and Annabelle told her that we weren't what we looked like and that they'd talk about it later. And weeks ago, when we talked about writing, she was very quick to accept after I offered to read her book."

"You think she's using you for your…connections?"

"It wouldn't be the first time. People have used me for what they can get out of me my whole life. I had a teacher in third grade give me a manuscript to bring to my dad. And who can forget Serena stepping on me to climb the ladder until she found someone that was better than me. I was so wrong about her, what makes me think I'm right about Annabelle? If she wants to be published, I'm the easiest route to get there."

Gabe didn't respond to the last comment. Maybe he'd gone too far. Sebastian knew deep down that Annabelle was not sleeping with him just to get a book deal. Yet here he was accusing her of just that to one of her closest friends.

"Sebastian, stop. You're so in your head that you can't find a way out. Better than you? You think that Serena found someone better than you?"

Sebastian's stomach rolled. Of course whoever she ended up was better than him. He couldn't prove himself to her, just like he couldn't to Annabelle.

Gabe continued when he didn't answer. "This is one of my closest friends you're talking about, and she's nothing like you're portraying her. If you gave off even an ounce of this doubt to her today, it's no wonder she was upset."

He couldn't respond to this either. Annabelle Winters had taken his confidence and threw it in the trashcan. Oh, he knew this wasn't Annabelle's fault, his own internal compass, the one that steered him in the right direction, was being rocked to the core.

"I'm sorry, Gabe. You're right."

"I know what you're going through, hell, I went through the ringer until I figured it out with Devlin."

As much as Sebastian needed Gabe's council, he was happy for a change of subject. "How are things going with you two now?"

Gabe glanced around the room like he expected the door to fly open, and when it stayed firmly shut, he pulled an object out of his pocket.

"My Grandma's ring," he explained. "I haven't told anyone of my plans yet, not even Grey, cause he'd tell Pru and the whole thing would get spoiled."

Happiness spread through his chest at Gabe's words. "That's such good news. When are you planning to propose?"

"I thought about doing it when we were at her cousin's wedding, but it didn't seem like the right time. Now we're almost to Grey and Pru's wedding and I don't want to overshadow their moment, so sometime in the fall, I think."

Sebastian stayed for a few more hours to help Gabe with some of the renovations he was working on, thankful for the distraction, but was thrown back into a mental tailspin after he left.

Sebastian heard everything Gabe said. Gabe had known Annabelle for a long time, after all, and he did trust his opinion. But. There was a but still hanging around in his head that he couldn't get rid of. What did that say about him that he'd throw around the word love so casually, yet he didn't think he could trust Annabelle?

One of the best days he'd had in his life had crashed and burned in such a spectacular fashion that he was having trouble separating his past from his present. He wasn't even sure if trust was the right word. He'd trusted Serena and he knew very well how that all ended.

He drove through the countryside, all his windows down, letting the breeze do its best job at clearing his head. What was Annabelle doing to him? Hell, what was this town doing to him? Being sent to Amber Falls was never meant to be a permanent assignment, the workload that continued to build up in Atlanta was a testament to that, and he realized he'd been treating this whole newspaper business like it was the only thing on his plate. He was tired of thinking something was wrong with him, and he needed to get his life back under control.

Sebastian slid his phone into his car's phone mount and pressed the on button. The time for him to go back to his real life was here. One where he didn't see cows on his daily commute or worry about how soon he'd need to get snow tires on his Benz.

A series of beeps, chimes and tones crashed him hard back to Earth. He was Sebastian Locke, Atlanta media mogul, not some backwater newspaper editor that cared about peach pie bake-offs. He tapped the button to listen to the most recent of his many voicemails.

"Sebastian, it's Tim. We've been trying to get ahold of you all day, where are you?" The voice of Locke Communications' head lawyer came through the phone. "The deal with Poppers Network is falling through and we need you back ASAP, like we needed you here this morning. Call me back."

Chapter Twenty-One

Annabelle hadn't seen Sebastian for almost a week. Six days and eighteen hours if she was precise.

After the disaster that was the flea market, she'd wanted to take the weekend to be by herself and evaluate where they were going. Her reluctance to introduce him to her mom, followed by his same behavior with Brenda made her question what either of them wanted.

Then, when she got to work Monday morning, she opened her email to a company-wide memo from the boss.

Dear Bee Staff,
I've been called back to Atlanta.
I don't know how long I'll be gone, so follow your typical escalation path and if there's anything that can't be resolved I'll jump in.
I know there have been some questions about the 4th of July, so I'd like you to know that you all will have the day off, paid.
Sebastian Locke

She almost vomited when she read the first line, then had to run to the bathroom after the last. Annabelle sat on the floor in a stall of the Amber Falls Bee bathroom, ill at the thought of not seeing Sebastian again.

This is where Prudence found her a short time later.

"AB?" Prudence's voice floated through the sterile space.

"I'm in here." Annabelle slammed the lid of the toilet, confident that she wasn't going to lose her breakfast anymore.

"I figured that." There was a pause. "Why are you in here?"

Annabelle left the stall and walked to the sink, splashing water over her face.

"I was sick to my stomach, but I'm okay now."

Prudence's eyes widened. "You're not pregnant, are you?"

"Oh, Jesus, no, I'm not." She held out her hand. "Grab me a towel, will you?"

"Yeah, if you tell me what the hell is going on. No one could find you. Your purse and phone are on your desk and your laptop is open."

"You didn't snoop before you came to find me?"

"*I'm* not the reporter. My first thought was to find my missing friend, not to get a story."

Annabelle opened the bathroom door and walked back to her office, and Prudence followed her.

"I only ever did that once, and you were fine the whole time." She motioned for Prudence to sit in her extra chair, then eased into hers and flipped her laptop around. "Sebastian sent this."

She waited in silence while Prudence read the short note, barely meeting her eyes when she was done.

"And this means what, exactly, to you?"

Annabelle shrugged. "We sort of got into a fight last week. At least I think it was a fight."

"Usually couples know what a fight is."

"Are we a couple, though? Or two people sleeping with each other?"

Prudence slowly nodded. "I think I see where this is going. My mom mentioned she ran into you at the flea market this weekend, does it have anything to do with that?"

"My mom was there, too."

"Ooof. What happened?"

"Sebastian and I were having a good time just being together and LuAnne shows up asking me if gave my book to Sebastian to read." She continued after Prudence's exclamation. "Then I dropped his hand and acted like I've never talked about my book or him with my mom before."

"You have, though?"

"Against my will. You know how LuAnne is. But, I hadn't told her that Sebastian and I were more than just workmates and I don't think she liked that. Thank God Shirley was there, otherwise we'd still be there answering my mom's questions."

"I should've brought coffee," was Prudence's reply.

"I'm surprised you didn't, actually."

"I'll only make this mistake once."

Annabelle sat back in her chair with a huff. "That's not all that happened. After that we ran into some woman, you know Brenda from the realtor's office? Brenda insinuated that they'd slept together and then he introduced me as his employee."

"Yikes."

"Yikes is right." Prudence cocked her head. "Didn't you kind of do the same thing to him with your mom?"

"I don't know." Annabelle buried her head in her hands. "I asked him to drop me off at home and that we'd talk later, but every time I tried to type a text to him over the weekend, I didn't know what to say. Did I want to apologize, or get into a fight? Was I going to accuse him of being ashamed of me or that he was with an employee? Every one of those thoughts ran through my head and I didn't like any of them, so I just didn't say anything and now he's gone."

"You gave him a chance and that turned out okay, right?"

"I guess, for the whole week we were together."

"Listen, AB. None of us could understand how much animosity you had for him until he was here, then you fight for months until you start sleeping together. And shortly after that you cut him off, so you can't be mad at him for avoiding you this week. Even I have whiplash from the turnaround you two did. You need to give him the same grace you'd give any of us and just talk to him and find out what's going on."

Annabelle tried to absorb what Prudence said. They had done a quick U-turn and it seemed like neither of them were prepared for the consequences.

"I don't know what's going on in his life, that's pretty clear by the way he left. We'd just started opening up to each other and then my mom went and screwed it up. Do you remember when I told you once in college that my mom would ruin my life?"

"Yeah, because she made you get a job to pay for your spring break trip to Aruba sophomore year in college?"

"Well, she's done it."

"Don't be so quick to throw her under the bus. This is your life and you control it, not her."

"Stay away from me with all your logic, I just want to wallow."

"I'm not going to let you. He's going to show back up here one day, maybe even for the picnic, and if you don't figure this out, you're going to fall back into old habits — and no one wants that to happen."

"Neither do I."

"Then do something about it."

"What am I going to say? At least if I still hated him I could throw insults and not care, but now, it's different, I have to *care* about how he feels."

"You know that you don't have to, you can call it all off and say you tried and it didn't work, that's your choice."

"That's not how love works."

These words settled over them like a blanket of fog.

"You know what you just said, right? I didn't even have to rapid fire question you."

"Dammit!"

"I don't think you should be reacting like this."

"It's the only acceptable way to react to admitting I'm in love with Sebastian Locke."

"You know what? I believe you. C'mon, get it out of your system, so when you tell him you don't make it seem like loving him is tantamount to having the plague."

"No, I'm fine now. But how am I going to tell him if he's not here?"

"If only we had a small handheld device that could connect you to him no matter the distance. Wouldn't that be nice?"

"Ugh, fine. Go away so I can call him."

"There's my Annabelle. Now don't screw this up."

* * * *

Sebastian missed a call from Annabelle. She'd texted once after he left, but he hadn't replied. Not out of spite, but working nonstop on keeping this deal from falling through had taken every ounce of his energy, leaving him spent for the few hours of sleep he was able to get each night.

She'd called the night before he was going to fly back to Amber Falls and he ached with the need to hear her voice, but what he wanted to say he had to say in person. He didn't want to give her a chance to break his heart from one thousand miles away.

Now, standing at the edge of the Amber Falls park, watching Annabelle Winters play with Renee's daughter, Eva, he knew he'd made the right choice. The only thing he needed to do was to convince her to take him back.

A good number of partiers followed him with their eyes as he walked across the grass to Annabelle. Her back was to him, though, and he stood a moment, taking in everything he could about her.

"Winters."

Annabelle stilled, then set Eva on the ground and turned.

"Sir."

"I'm sorry I didn't call back."

She raised one eyebrow. "That's what you're sorry about?"

"You're going to make this hard on me, aren't you?"

"Would you expect anything else?"

Sebastian motioned with his head for her to follow him. "I'm sure we can have an entire conversation where we ask each other questions back and forth, but let's do it away from the crowd?"

Annabelle nodded and followed behind. Sebastian didn't know where to go—there were people everywhere—and on a hail Mary he tried the door to Gabe's new shop and breathed a sigh of relief when it opened.

"I'm sure he won't mind us being in here." Sebastian closed the door after Annabelle came through.

They stood, neither of them moving or speaking for what could have been an eternity. He wanted to go first, to tell her how much he'd come to love her, but he needed to ask a question. The one question that plagued his brain and made him question his sanity.

"Are you using me to get a book published?"

"You have got to be kidding me." Annabelle punched him in the shoulder. "You're the one that wanted to know what I was working on and wanted to read my stuff. I would never have asked you that, I'm fully prepared to do it on my own. In fact, I tried to not talk to you about it at all because I didn't want you to think this exact thing."

The relief that flowed through Sebastian at these words was so intense he thought he would pass out.

"What about your Mom?"

"What about her?"

"You know what. Her comments at the flea market about giving me your book?"

"She thinks she's on a first name basis with the First Lady, her comments mean nothing."

Sebastian's hopes lifted now that she was joking with him, but Annabelle wasn't done letting him have it yet.

"I am sorry for my part in how we ended things that day, but I can't believe you'd leave town like that. You packed up and left without a word to me. I know we don't know how to fight like a couple, but you could've just talked to me if that's how you were feeling."

"No, I couldn't! That's what I've been trying to tell you. You have no clue what you do to me, how you affect me. My life is about control and when I'm with you, I lose all of it. There's only one person who could upend my life and make me question everything. You."

He reached out and took her hands, pulling her close to him.

"I remember the first day I met you. Serena had just broken up with me and here you come, waltzing into my office and I thought, great, another woman who wants something from me. Yet another person that sees only Sebastian Locke, publisher, and not me. Not the man that I am and the person I want to be."

"Oh, Sebastian," Annabelle whispered.

"When I saw you again here, I felt the same. That day came rushing back to me and how I delt with you in Amber Falls stemmed from that, and that alone. Then, after we got together I thought you were yet another person I had to prove myself to—my dad, the company, the people of Amber Falls—but I didn't give you enough credit that you never made me feel *unworthy* even when I couldn't stop thinking that something was wrong with me."

"There's nothing wrong with you, Sebastian. Women like that, the ones who use everyone around them for their own gain, will get their comeuppance."

"I don't want revenge, I just want to be free of them."

"You can be. You are. As long as you're with me, you'll never have to question your worth again."

Then it clicked. He'd thought Annabelle had been holding something back from him all this time — because she had been.

"I feel like a fool. This whole time I thought you were keeping something from me, and my mind went to a dark place. You *were* holding something back, an important part of yourself, because you were so worried about my precious ego and that I would think I was being used. You couldn't talk about writing with me *because* of me."

"I knew you'd been used for your connections your whole life and I didn't want you to think that I was like any of those people."

"None of them compare to you. Even with your arguing and competitiveness and your—"

"Hey, I thought you liked me?"

"Oh, the irony of words not working for the publisher." He pulled her tightly to him and lowered his head. "Fine, I'll show you."

Epilogue

Annabelle walked down the aisle toward Sebastian. She wasn't wearing white, rather black, just like the avenging angel he preferred. In this one instant the rest of his life flashed through his eyes. A house in the country with a white picket fence, five kids, two dogs and a cat and chickens in the backyard. Then, an empty nest, but now filled with grandchildren, so many that you couldn't hear a word anyone was saying, but Sebastian loved the noise. Annabelle was graying at her temples, a shimmering silver that complemented her dark locks. She was smiling, so big that he thought she'd never stop, and he never wanted her to.

He was restless, wanting her to be walking toward him for their wedding, for the start of their life. He'd waited a lifetime for Annabelle Winters, and he didn't want to wait any longer. But wait he must. This was his friend's day, and he wanted to be completely present for it. So, he meant to pay attention to the ceremony, he really did, but Annabelle was the only person he saw, the only thing that would matter to him for the rest of his life. He'd propose right now, stop the ceremony and drop to one knee if he didn't want her to run for the hills.

After the ceremony they danced, kissed and danced some more. She'd taken a break from him to dance with Gabe and he was sitting at a table with his sister, lounging back in his tux, his bow tie undone, sipping on champagne.

"I like that you're back, Sofia. I've come to love Amber Falls and it feels more like home when my sister is here."

"I was surprised that I missed this little town as much as I did the last time I left."

"Wyatt said you did great with summer stock, and that the costumes were a hit because of you."

"I had a lot of fun helping. Maybe they can use me next year."

"I hope so, I'll take any excuse to have you back here."

"Speaking of that. Greyson mentioned that the college needs someone to guest lecture next semester. I thought that with my BFA in fashion, I'd be able to interview for the position."

Sebastian saw Greyson at the table next to them chatting with a rather stuffy looking man, dark hair just a little longer than fashionable with a beard just as dark.

"Hey, Grey, you trying to help me keep my sister in town, too?"

"I wouldn't be keeping her here, she would be deciding to stay. The college would be lucky to have her." Greyson gestured to the man next to him. "In fact, this is Liam MacKanzie, a history professor."

Sebastian noticed the long stare between Sofia and Liam.

"We've met," Sofia finally spoke, while Liam just nodded, looking stuffier, if that was even possible.

"Hey, you." Annabelle came up to the table and sat on Sebastian's lap. "You wanna dance before Prudence throws the bouquet?"

"It's almost bouquet time?" Greyson stood. "I'd better go find Pru."

Sebastian smiled an apology at Sofia as Annabelle led him away. It would do Sofia good to talk to someone who didn't seem like quite the free spirit she was, the opposite it seemed.

They swayed on the dance floor while the ladies gathered at one end in anticipation of the bridal tradition of catching the bouquet and being named the next woman to get married.

"You're not going to throw your hat in the ring?"

"No. That's for single ladies. I'm very taken."

"Hell yeah, you're very taken."

He tightened his arms around Annabelle and kept swaying even though the music had stopped, and the countdown started. Once Prudence threw the bouquet over her shoulder, there was a moment where it was suspended in mid-air while a dozen women held their hands up, hoping to be named the next bride. He was surprised when he saw Sofia was the victor, then watched as she stumbled on her heels, falling to one side before she was caught by Liam. Liam held Sofia in his arms, appearing to steady her.

"That's one second too long man. One second too long," Sebastian muttered under his breath, watching the situation unfold.

"Sebastian, was he just gazing longingly into her eyes?" Annabelle joked.

Sebastian growled. "What?"

"Leave her alone, she's a grown woman who doesn't need her older brother breathing down her neck, especially if he wants her to stay in town."

"But he's still got his arms around her."

Annabelle turned him toward her and ran a hand down his cheek. "Have I told you how handsome you look in that tux?"

Sebastian smiled, everything else forgotten. He was with the love of his life, he had a ring in his pocket to propose when the time was right, and he was surrounded by the best group of friends a man could ask for.

Amber Falls had been good to him, after all.

Sign up for our newsletter and find out about all our romance book releases, eBook sales and promotions, sneak peeks and FREE romance books!

Fallbank: Make Me Fall
Cass Scotka

Excerpt

The burst of crisp air lifted the hairs on the nape of Bridget's neck. She glanced toward the opening door as the bell above it chimed, and smiled out of habit. She froze her muscles in place as an old schoolmate who used to tease her walked in. "Hey, Julie. What brings you in today?" She knit her fingers together to keep from fidgeting.

Julie beelined her way. "Bridget! I'm glad it's you here today. Not that your gran isn't lovely, it's just that I'm hoping you can help me. You did assist me that one other time."

As if she could forget Julie wanting a love potion from her. She fought the urge to roll her eyes. Instead, Bridget tucked her dark curls behind one ear. "Of course, what do you need?"

Julie leaned in closer and glanced around furtively, despite no other customers being present. "Something for nausea," she whispered and touched a palm to her abdomen. "Because…you know."

She sucked in a surprised breath and widened her eyes. "You're pregnant?" Bridget kept her voice soft and cut her eyes over to the door for a split second.

Nodding, Julie beamed. "It's still early and we're going to wait to tell anyone, but the morning sickness is killing me." Her diamond ring glinted in the light as she brushed her bangs to the side. "It's been a rough couple of weeks since I found out. I thought since you had something for attracting Ben, then you might have something now?"

Uncomfortable warmth smoldered in Bridget's chest. "No, no. The lotion I gave you wasn't for attraction. It was for confidence. Lavender for relaxation, ylang-ylang to boost romantic thoughts and rosehips for feminine allure. All combined to give confidence in yourself. A natural inner glow is what attracts someone, not the lotion you put on. Soft skin and smelling good boosts self-assurance. Nothing more." She spun and stepped to the back wall with Julie trailing along.

"Whatever you say." Julie laughed and waved a hand. "All that matters is that you have something to solve my morning sickness problem."

Bridget snagged a tub from the third shelf in front of her then led the way to the left wall and picked up a tin. "Here you go." She held both out. "Lotion to put on pressure points when you're feeling nauseated. Rub it into those spots, and the massage plus the scent should help lessen it."

Julie examined the containers as Bridget continued talking.

"Tea to help keep things at bay. Ginger and lemongrass, plus caffeine-free." They crossed the well-loved dark wood floor over to the ornately carved mahogany counter with an heirloom cash register prominently displayed on it. Beside it rested a small white tablet and credit card reader. An assortment of colored leaves and tiny pumpkins dotted the length of the desk.

As Bridget rang up the items, she flashed a quick smile. "Hopefully these will ease your tummy troubles, but obviously I can't give any guarantees." She shrugged and opened her mouth to apologize, but Julie interrupted.

"Okay, whatever you say. I'll try anything at this point and even if it's just a little relief, I'll take it!" She tapped her card and grabbed the gold-embossed navy paper bag with her goods. "Thank you so much. I knew you'd have what I needed." She stepped back and arched one brow with a colder smile. "You're so magical." Julie turned back and headed out. "After all, you are the town witch!" Julie's laugh vibrated after her exit.

Bridget wanted to protest, but in the pit of her stomach, an icy void opened for a shaky moment. As Julie walked out of view, Bridget wiped her sweaty palms on her jeans and swallowed hard. "Not a witch. Not magical. I just sell herbal stuff. That's it."

Ugh, when would the people of this town learn? They never seemed to mind when they needed her products but wouldn't associate with her outside of the shop. To make herself feel less isolated, she shot off a quick text to her cousin, Becca, to see about grabbing dinner together this week.

Then she shook off her mutterings and anxiety, instead focusing on closing up the shop for the night. A quick sweeping of the floors, restocking gaps on the shelves and closing out the register and Bridget deemed herself ready to head home.

She poked her head out a side door and called up the stairs. "Gran, I'm heading home."

A lined face peeped into the hall. "Night, Bridgie! I'll open up in the morning and see you around midday."

Bridget furrowed her brow. "You sure? I don't mind coming in."

Gran waved her off. "Enjoy your morning. It's not as if I haven't been running this store for almost my entire life."

With a sigh, Bridget relented. There was no arguing when Gran made a decision. Like moving out of their little house together to live above the shop. Apparently, Gran wanted to live out her remaining years without a granddaughter "cramping her style" in case she had any "gentlemen callers." While Bridget couldn't fault her grandmother for wanting a bit of independence after raising two granddaughters, she still felt the sting. And the loneliness of the empty house.

"All right, Gran. I'll bring lunch then. Good night!"

"Night-night, dear."

After locking the front door, Bridget tucked her hand into the pockets of her hunter-green peacoat and walked up the block to the Harvest Street parking garage. The brisk fall wind lifted the heavy mass of long, dark curls from her shoulders. Tension released from her muscles as each step took her from Three Sisters Apothecary. She lifted her face to the evening sunlight, enjoying the warmth. Today had gone well. Sales were decent, the autumn decorations added a fresh breath of vibrancy and the customers were friendly...ish.

A beep from her phone revealed a response from Becca, suggesting Tuesday for dinner at her house. Happiness filled her chest as she smiled and sent back a message agreeing.

With September ushering in the pumpkin patches opening for the season and the leaves starting to turn, more and more tourists were trickling in. The upcoming annual harvest festival in two months would keep those numbers climbing. A grateful breath left her as a red truck rumbled down the road. She glanced at the brown-haired, bearded man inside the cab as he passed, but didn't recognize him. Maybe another tourist? New lumberjack in town for seasonal work?

A mother and child walked in her direction about half a block from her. Without thinking, Bridget lifted the corners of her mouth in greeting, but the woman took one look at her and jerked to halt. Then she tugged her child's hand and they scurried to the other side of the road.

The wind carried the child's voice. "Mommy, is that the witch?"

The woman rushed to quiet her son, but it was too late. Bridget's brief moment of confidence and contentment fizzled and died within her. She pulled the collar of her jacket tighter and tucked her chin into the fabric. Eyes down, she double-timed her steps to get to her car and get home. Alone.

* * * *

Jack scratched at his beard, still adjusting to having hair on his face, as he drove down the main road in Fallbank. What was he doing in the middle-of-nowhere Oregon again? Oh yeah, investigating whether this local logging company would be the next great acquisition for Thompson Incorporated. He tightened his fingers on the wheel of the red pick-up truck he'd purchased used as part of his "undercover boss" scheme. His grandfather's scheme. The one designed to "help find his path in life." Being groomed to take over the family business didn't count.

"I guess an MBA and landing all those deals for our current companies over the last five years isn't enough," he grumbled as he drove through the quaint downtown. All of the shops had fall-themed window displays and the sidewalks were lined with wooden flower boxes overflowing with chrysanthemums of all colors, with large pumpkins nestled between them. A massive sign stretched across two light poles advertising the "Forty-Third Annual Fallbank Fall Festival" on Halloween this year. Was that what counted as excitement around here? He shook his head. Well, at least this town wasn't completely devoid of any form of entertainment.

Jack had to admit a quieter pace for a few months would be a nice change from the high intensity of the office and hustle of Seattle. A way to reset the nagging sense of restlessness, of life slipping by with only shallow platitudes to show for it. Sure, money could buy a lot, but there was something missing from his life that Jack couldn't name.

The vehicle passed a woman in a dark green coat, then a mother and child duo. The kid waved as he drove by and Jack raised a hand in return. Maybe that was what was missing. Companionship. A relationship with a woman who didn't want him for his money and gilded last name, but for him as a person. As a partner in life. Not that he was going to find that here. He snorted. Nope, he was here to learn the logging business firsthand and see how it fit within the massive holdings of the family business.

Two lefts and one right turn later and his phone had successfully navigated him to the office of Timber Logging Company. Jack hopped out of his truck and walked in. A tall, lanky guy with glasses met him.

"Hey, I'm Cornelius. You must be Jack?"

Shaking his offered hand, Jack nodded. "That's me. Nice to meet you. Sorry I'm late, traffic getting out of Seattle was even more ridiculous than I expected."

Cornelius laughed. "Well, that's one thing you won't have to worry about here. So, you're the new hire, huh? Ever done logging before?"

Heat crept into his cheeks and Jack found himself grateful for his newly grown beard. "Uh, not really. I've worked construction, though. I'm hoping that will give me something to go off. I'm a quick learner."

Cornelius lifted his eyebrows but didn't show any other surprise. "We'll do our best to keep you alive as long as you do the same for the rest of us."

"I can agree to that." He glanced around at the dated office interior. Linoleum flooring, faux-wood paneling, plain drop ceiling and well-used furniture. No wonder his father was eager about this deal. The business clearly needed an infusion of funds. Except the offices would shift up to Seattle once bought and they would bring their own teams to do the logging. As he looked back at Cornelius, a small stab of guilt hit him in the gut. Jack shook it off. This was business, not personal.

"You have a place to stay, Jack? Need anything to get you settled?" Cornelius nudged his glasses up his nose.

Jack cleared his throat. "I'm staying at the local hotel while I find a place to rent. I've got a couple of leads to check out. I think I'll be set by the weekend."

"Good, good. Let me know if you need any leads or want suggestions for things to do around town. This time of year, the tourist traffic picks up because of the crisp weather and fall celebrations happening in the surrounding area. There's got to be at least two each weekend within a fifty-mile radius. And of course, we have our own at the end of October." He grinned wide. "Fallbank is famous for our festival and lumberjack competition. Some great competitive games we've hosted. The festival boasts the largest turnout in the state for the last ten years since TLC sponsors it in conjunction with the fair." Cornelius waggled his brows. "The ladies love it."

Jack laughed with him and shook his head. "That'll be a sight to see. Who knows, maybe I'll have learned enough to enter a beginners' tournament. Although I'm not on the relationship market at the moment."

Cornelius hummed with a nod. "You have a girlfriend back in Seattle?"

"Nah, just taking a break after the last one." A year-long break, but who was counting?

"I hear you. I must admit, the fawning is nice. A little ego boost is never a bad thing."

"Right. Well, what time should I show up tomorrow? And where?"

Cornelius ran a hand through his sandy-blond hair. "I'd say around eight o'clock and you can meet me here. We usually ride up in teams with the equipment trucks."

"Sounds good." Jack nodded once more. "I'll see you tomorrow then."

"See you."

Back in town, Jack checked into the larger of the two hotels offered in Fallbank and crashed out on the bed. The hard mattress had him rethinking if he should have stayed at one of the multitudes of B&Bs around the area instead. He shook the thought off. He had several rentals to check out in the next two days so he could suck it up until he found a more permanent option. With that in mind, Jack set an alarm on his phone and closed his eyes. Travel weariness settled in his bones and in no time, he was out.

About the Authors

Rachael Heinan

Rachael's love of books started at a young age. Her love of romance novels started in university when she couldn't stand to read another textbook and picked up her first pure romance.

Rachael co-authors with Kimberly Metcalf. They met in the corporate world and their friendship flowed seamlessly into the real world.

Rachael lives in Minnesota, USA with her husband, daughter and four cats.

Kimberly Metcalf

Kimberly is an avid reader who managed to convince her best friend they could put their stories on paper. She is so excited to share them with you.

Based in North Dakota, USA, when not writing she can be found spending time with her family, cooking, or curled up in her favorite armchair with a book.

Rachael and Kimberly love to hear from readers. You can find their contact information, website details and author profile page at https://www.firstforromance.com

ENTWINED PUBLISHING